DOCTOR WHO
THE AWAKENING

For Pat, Susannah
and David, with love

DOCTOR WHO
THE AWAKENING

Based on the BBC television serial by Eric Pringle by arrangement with the British Broadcasting Corporation

ERIC PRINGLE

W.H. ALLEN · LONDON
1985

Novelisation copyright © Eric Pringle 1985
Original script copyright © Eric Pringle 1984
'Doctor Who' series copyright © British Broadcasting Corporation 1984, 1985

The BBC producer of *The Awakening*
was John Nathan-Turner,
the director was Michael Owen Morris.

Printed and bound in Great Britain by
Mackays of Chatham Ltd, Kent
for the Publishers, W.H. Allen & Co. PLC
44 Hill Street, London W1X 8LB

ISBN 0 491 03194 7

CONTENTS

1

An Unexpected Aura

Somewhere, horses' hooves were drumming the ground.

The woman's name was Jane Hampden, and that noise worried her. She was a schoolteacher, but just now her village school and its unwilling pupils were far from her thoughts: her mind raced with problems and uncertainties, making her head ache; she felt that if she did not share them with someone soon, she would go mad.

Jane was looking for farmer Ben Wolsey, but she could not find him anywhere. That was another problem, because time was short, and there were horses coming.

It was Jane's belief that the village of Little Hodcombe was being torn apart. She felt instinctively that those horses had something to do with it, like the recent bursts of violence and the cries and shouts which so frequently disturbed the peaceful countryside. She was sure, too, that the mysterious disappearance of her old friend Andrew Verney was connected in some way.

And there was another thing which bothered her, which she found more difficult to put into words. In a quiet, remote place like Little Hodcombe, tucked away as it was deep in the lush Dorset hinterland, far away from cities or politics or any sort of world-shattering event, it was as normal as daylight that everybody should know pretty well everything about everybody else: you didn't mind your own business here so much as you minded other people's. Jane was no different from the rest in this respect, and yet suddenly she felt that she didn't know anything any more.

All at once, the place and its people seemed somehow strange, as if that normal, everyday life of thatched houses and quiet corners and fields and streams which composed Little Hodcombe was slipping away and being replaced by a new, nameless void, which contained only premonitions, and fears, and noises like this distant jingle of harness and the beating of those hooves on the baked earth.

Jane hurried through Ben Wolsey's farmyard, searching for him and pondering on these things. She knew it must be nonsense – that perhaps she really was going mad – yet it seemed to her that the simple rules which governed daily living, basic things like the fact that today is reliably today and not tomorrow or yesterday, and that what is past and dead and gone really is so, no longer applied so firmly as they used to do. The behaviour of ordinary people was becoming extraordinary, and unpredictable, and strange.

Nobody believed her when she told them her fears. They thought she was just being silly; that she was a nuisance and a killjoy. And it was equally useless for Jane to tell herself that she was deluded, and that these were fantasies quite unfit for a forward-looking young schoolteacher in 1984. She pretended twenty times a day that everything was as it should be. She looked out at Little Hodcombe and it was manifestly the same as it had always been; it smelt the same as it always had, and when she touched its buildings for reassurance they felt as they must have felt for centuries.

And yet she *knew* that it wasn't the same.

How, though, could she possibly make anyone believe her when she was uncertain what had happened and couldn't find the words to describe how she felt? But she was determined to make this one last attempt. She would

8

get Ben Wolsey, who had always been a staunch friend, on to her side – surely Ben, the burly down-to-earth farmer that he was, would listen to her, and try to understand.

Unless, of course, the sickness had got to him too. He was not to be found, and those horses were coming closer by the second. Jane felt the vibrations of their hooves under her feet, trembling through the clay of the farmyard which had dried hard as brown concrete over weeks of unusually hot sun and cloudless blue skies. This constant sunlight was abnormal in England. It made her dizzy. It dazzled her now with its harsh bright glare on the weathered red brick and blue paintwork of the farm buildings which enclosed the yard. It warmed her head as she hurried from one building to another, calling for the absent farmer, moving from barn to byre to implement shed, looking into doorways where the glare ended in a sharp black line of shadow.

'Ben?' she shouted.

She stood on tiptoe and looked over a stable door into the inky blackness of a shed, but the darkness was like a wall and she could see nothing. There was no reply. Listening for sounds of movement, she heard insects murmuring in the heat, vibrating the air. And nothing else.

Jane brought her head back out into the sunlight. The air out here was vibrating too, with the chatter of unseen birds. Suddenly she felt uneasy. She hummed quietly to cheer herself up and hurried on to the next building.

She was a small, attractive woman, neat in white shirt and grey waistcoat, green corduroy jeans and boots. She wore her hair tied up in a bun, to make her look taller than she really was; wisps of it hung loosely about her forehead. She carried a green knitted jacket slung casually over her shoulder in case the breeze which now and then fanned the farmyard should grow into something stronger: with the English climate, even in the middle of a drought you could never be sure.

She was no longer sure of anything.

Again Jane stood on tiptoe to peer over another stable door into another black hole. 'Ben!' she asked of the murky interior. Again it swallowed up her voice, and returned nothing except the whine and whirr of swarming flies.

But the horses were coming. In the yard the noise of their hooves was stronger and the vibrations were more distinct. Jane was sure she could hear harness jingling; the breeze which flipped the loose strands of hair on her forehead brought rhythmic clashing sounds to her ears. Worried, she pushed her hair back into place, thrust her hands into her pockets and ran to another doorway.

'Are you there, Ben?' she demanded. There was no response here either; she was alone with the disembodied sounds of unseen insects, birds and horses. It was uncanny.

And then, suddenly it was more than sounds. They were coming very fast – big heavy horses making the earth throb with the hammer blows of their feet, and they seemed to take over the world. Jane could no longer hear insects or birds, she was aware only of this one stream of noise bearing down on her.

And now there were voices too, rising above the hooves, men's shouts encouraging the horses and spurring them to even greater speed. Startled, Jane moved across the farmyard to look out between the buildings at the surrounding countryside.

Like everything else, it seemed that the usually placid green landscape of fields and trees and hedgerows had altered its character. Instead of a gently pastoral scene it had become a page from her school history books: the seventeenth century was moving towards her across a field, thundering out of the misty past in the shape of three horses – two chestnuts flanking a grey – and riders

10

flushed with the excitement and danger of the English Civil War.

They came abreast of one another. The horseman on the left had the broad, plumed hat and extravagantly embroidered clothing of a Cavalier of King Charles the First; the other two wore battledress – the steel breast-plates and helmets of mounted troopers. The middle rider, on the big grey horse, carried a brightly coloured banner.

They were an awe-inspiring sight. With her hands on her hips and her mouth open in amazement, Jane watched them approach the farm. When they neared the buildings the rider on the left spurred his horse and galloped ahead of the others. He came through the gap between the farm buildings; as he entered the farmyard and approached Jane he slowed to a canter. She had a clear view of a sharp-featured face, with waxed moustache, pointed beard and shoulder-length wig under the great nodding peacock feather which adorned his hat. He was the perfect image of a seventeenth-century Cavalier.

Jane was speechless. The Cavalier cantered past her with a supercilious stare. Now the troopers were in the farmyard too; their horses' hooves clattered on the baked clay earth. They also passed by, paying her no heed at all.

Then something odd happened, as frightening as it was unexpected. The troopers wheeled their horses around to face Jane. The rider on the grey horse lowered his banner and pointed it straight at her, like a lance. And suddenly without warning he shouted and urged his horse into action. The point of the banner swept forward. They gathered speed, looming at Jane out of the shimmering heat of the enclosed farmyard.

Jane felt her stomach muscles contract with fear. Her open-mouthed wonder turned to disbelief at the sight of the lunging horse and its rider thundering towards her.

11

All her senses concentrated on the banner; her whole attention narrowed to that single point of steel which held firm and steady, and pointed at her body like a skewer.

This can't be happening, she thought, it's impossible. Yet the point came on, propelled by horses' hooves and rider's shouts. She began to run.

'Aaargh!' the trooper screamed. His horse tossed its head; its nostrils flared and its hooves bit into the ground and brought up clouds of dust. 'There's no sense in this,' the logical side of Jane's mind was protesting, but at the same time her instinct for self-preservation was working flat out, and with only a split second to spare she threw herself against a wall, pressing her body into its rough stone.

The lance swept harmlessly past her and the hooves pounded by. She was momentarily aware of a stern, steel-helmeted face glaring at her, and then it, too, passed on.

'Don't be so stupid!' she screamed after the rider. 'You'll kill somebody!'

Her chest heaving, Jane moved away from the wall to look for the other riders. She tried to control her temper and the trembling which had suddenly afflicted her frame. As her eyes searched the yard the sunlight dazzled them, the heat shimmered at her from sky and earth and walls, and everything seemed unreal. Everything, that is, except the sharp, glistening steel point of the lance, which, unbelievably, was coming back at her.

The trooper, after he had passed her by the first time, had raised the lance and turned it back into a banner, and galloped to the far side of the farmyard. Roughly he wheeled his horse around and steadied it, and himself. Then he yelled, lowered the banner and charged again.

The bewilderment and distress Jane was feeling chilled suddenly to the realisation that this man really was trying to harm her. The hooves thundered and once

more the fiercely pointed lance thrust through the
the farmyard towards her. Drawing in her breath sha:
ply, Jane ran again. This time she threw herself into the
open doorway of a barn. She dived inside just as lance,
horse and rider swept over the spot where she had been
standing.

It was cool in the barn. It was dark, too, after the
brilliant sunshine outside, although there were shafts of
light where the sun pierced through cracks in roof and
wall. It smelt cool and musty, with that peculiar sour-
sweet smell that old barns have, where animals have lain
and produce has been stored for hundreds of years.

It was indeed a very old barn, so old it was beginning
to crumble. The interior was ramshackle in the extreme:
the stone-flagged floor was strewn with barrels, fodder,
oddments of machinery, bales of hay, drums of oil,
cabbages, turnips and potatoes and all the bits and
pieces of tackle that a farmer had found useful once and
might do so again one day. Jane had often thought that
Ben Wolsey knew less than half of what was stored in
this barn, either strewn across the broad, dark floor or
stacked on the upper level, an unsafe gallery reached by
a set of open, rickety wooden steps.

Now, as the trooper charged past the door and she
tumbled inside, that thick, musty smell made her nose
itch and the instant darkness blinded her eyes. Bewildered and trembling, she staggered over to a spot where
some sacks were strewn on the floor beside a heap of
vegetables. She sat down on the sacks, in a narrow pool
of sunlight. Here she propped her elbows on her knees
and her head in her hands and tried to gather her senses
together. Outside she could hear the heavy prancing and
scraping of horses' hooves, which meant that her ass-
ailants were still around.

They would come in here at any moment. She tried to
think what to do, but before any constructive idea
occurred to her a black shadow reached out of the

13

ess and swooped over her body. Startled again, Jane looked up – and gasped at the sight of a huge man striding across the barn towards her.

This man, too, was equipped for war, dressed in a Roundhead uniform which had turned him into one of Oliver Cromwell's dreaded Ironshirts. An orange sash lent a vivid splash of colour to the predominantly grey appearance of his leather doublet, steel breastplate and great knee boots; his head was enclosed in a heavy steel helmet and his face obscured by the frame of his visor. He reached Jane before she could move, an armoured giant stooping over her out of the darkness of the barn.

'Don't touch me!' she gasped.

Her body tensed. She tried to back away from those long arms, but there was no escaping their reach and she felt herself being lifted into the air as effortlessly as if she had been made of thistledown.

'Get off me!' she shouted.

To her surprise, the man put her down lightly on her feet, stepped back, removed his helmet and tucked it under his arm. A red, burly face smiled benignly at her. 'It's only me,' he said.

His voice was gentle, his eyes were mild, and a smile creased his face. Jane had found Ben Wolsey at last.

'Ben!' She almost sobbed with relief. But the sight of his uniform shocked her. It meant that he too had joined the general insanity, and it was hard for her to reconcile the soft-mannered, pleasant farmer she thought she knew, with this seventeenth-century killer. There was no sense in it. 'Ben,' she said, 'you're mad.'

The farmer smiled that good-humoured, slightly mocking smile of his. 'Nonsense, my dear,' he said. 'It's just a bit of fun.'

Of course he wouldn't listen. He was just like the rest of them, Jane thought; it was worse than driving knowledge into her unwilling pupils.

'Fun!' she shouted at him. The memory of her experience in the farmyard was still searingly fresh: where was the fun in being skewered against a wall? What fun was it watching grown, twentieth-century men dressing up to recreate an old war and tearing a village to pieces in the process?

But before she could protest the barn door flew open and two men were momentarily silhouetted against the light – two of the three men who had just given her the fright of her life. They marched inside.

The leader was the Cavalier who had glared at Jane from his horse, and then blandly watched his trooper having his 'fun'. Sir George Hutchinson, Lord of the Manor of Little Hodcombe, owned half of the village and never allowed his tenants to forget it. He was a throwback to the old-fashioned arrogant squire, a dapper, military man with a brisk, authoritative manner that brooked no opposition. His assumed role of Royalist General now gave him unbounded opportunities for power and display, and Jane could see he was in his element. He strutted across the barn like a gaudy peacock, looking almost foppish with his long gloves and broad white lace collar, which overlaid a steel shield around his throat, and his bright red Royalist sash.

Stalking along behind Sir George was the predominantly dark figure of his land agent and general henchman, Joseph Willow. He was the trooper with the banner who had very nearly speared Jane – a man for whom these opportunities for violence were too tempting to ignore. He, too, wore the red Royalist sash. Florid and quick-tempered, he made an uncertain friend and a cruel enemy. Now he looked at Jane with a smug, triumphant expression.

With a single dramatic gesture Sir George removed his feathered hat and swept it through the air in a grandiose bow. It was a movement of supreme arrogance. Added to the complacent smirk on Willow's face,

15

it was too much for Jane's shattered patience. Before the country squire could utter a word, she flew at him.

'Sir George, you must stop these war games,' she demanded.

'Why?' His eyes dilated with mock surprise. 'Miss Hampden, you of all people – our schoolteacher – should appreciate the value of re-enacting actual events. It's a living history!' Behind the mildness of his manner his gleaming eyes were sharp as needles.

But Jane had been blessed with a forceful character of her own. She was not to be cowed by Sir George's position – civil or military – nor by those obsessive eyes. 'It's getting out of hand,' she insisted. 'The village is in turmoil.'

Sir George glanced sideways at his henchman, and laughed. 'So there's been a little damage,' he smiled, dismissing it as a trifle. 'Well, that's the way people used to behave in those days.' He marched past Jane and Wolsey and strode among the bales and fodder to sit on the steps to the gallery. There he looked like a judge passing sentence – or, in this case, exoneration. 'It's a game,' he explained. 'You must expect high spirits.'

As if to emphasise this point he reached inside the folds of his tunic and produced a black, spongy substance rolled into a ball. He kneaded it in his fingers, and tossed it into the air and caught it again.

'It's not a game when people get hurt,' Jane argued. 'It must stop.'

'And so it shall. We have but one last battle to fight.' Sir George regarded her with eyes that glinted obsessively. He tossed the spongy ball and caught it, and when he spoke again he weighed his words very carefully, and used his most authoritative and deliberate manner. 'Join us,' he suggested. 'See the merit of what we do.'

He fixed her now with a steely stare. There was an unnatural brightness about him which made Jane shiver;

16

his eyes seemed, like the point of that lance, to be trying to pin her to the wall. She found his invitation easy to resist.

The steady hum of machinery in the console room of the TARDIS proclaimed that the time-machine's advanced but often tired technology was for once in reasonable working order. Or appeared to be – its occupants were keenly aware that at any given moment any number of things might, unknown to them, be going wrong. For that reason constant checking and running repairs were matters of permanent priority.

That was why Turlough was now sprawled on his back, probing at an illuminated panel on the underside of the console. A red light flashed in his eyes and bleeps from the console whined in his ears. He prodded the panel again and looked out to where the Doctor was performing his own bit of maintenance on some circuit boards.

'Is that any better?' he asked.

The Doctor examined the monitor screen. He frowned, and flicked a bank of switches. Immediately the console screamed, making a high-pitched whining, warbling noise like an animal in pain.

'No,' he replied. He watched the time rotor jerk erratically up and down: things were definitely not any better. 'There's some time distortion,' he added.

Tegan, who had been watching their efforts with amused curiosity, knew the TARDIS's tricks of old, and references to distortions of any kind were enough to set alarm bells ringing in her head. Fully attentive now, she eyed the twitching time rotor suspiciously, detected a suppressed anxiety in the Doctor's manner and snapped, 'Is there a problem? We are going to Earth?'

The Doctor gave her a pained look to show how much he deplored her lack of faith. 'The place, date and time asked for,' he confirmed, as he moved on to examine

17

another set of instruments. 'How else could you visit your grandfather?'

How else indeed, Tegan wondered. She marvelled at the Doctor's ability to clear his mind of past mistakes and broken promises. His latest promise, to take her to visit her grandfather at his home in Little Hodcombe, England in the Earth year of 1984, demanded a precision of timing and placing which she sometimes believed to be quite beyond the TARDIS's capacity.

Now, though, Turlough echoed the Doctor's confidence. He crawled out from his cramped working quarters to check the monitor dials. 'We're nearly there,' he confirmed.

'You see?' The Doctor glared at her. But there was no time for him to enjoy his little triumph, because there was a sudden remarkable increase in the agitation of the time rotor. That in turn heralded an extreme turbulence which buffeted and shook the TARDIS like an earthquake. Lights flashed, the rotor shuddered, the room swayed and jolted, and its occupants had to cling to the console to avoid being dashed to the floor. For a moment or two they were shaken about like puppets and then, as suddenly as it began, the disturbance ceased.

The time rotor slowed, sank and became still. Its lights dimmed and extinguished. Where all had been noise and violent quivering there was now stillness and peace. Feeling their feet steady on the floor, they let go of the console.

'Well,' the Doctor gasped. 'We've arrived!'

'We hit an energy field.' Turlough's face was grim.

The Doctor nodded agreement. 'An unexpected aura for a quiet English village.'

Tegan was uncertain whether that remark was intended as a question, a suggestion or a hint that yet again plans had gone wrong. Despairing, she wanted to scream. 'Goodbye Grandfather,' she thought.

As if to confirm her suspicions the Doctor operated the

scanner screen and the shield rose to reveal a scene outside of far more violent upheaval than the shaking the TARDIS had suffered.

They seemed to have landed inside some kind of wide cellar, or possibly a crypt: all was gloom and shadow. Whatever it was, it was falling apart. They gained an impression of pillars and arches stretching away, and an earth floor heaped with rubble, but it was only a fleeting glimpse before everything was obscured by an avalanche of masonry which tumbled down and raised a plume of dust. This had only just begun to settle when the place shook again; blocks of stone cascaded down and rolling clouds of dust blotted out the view.

It looked like an earthquake out there. It was nothing like the sequestered haven which Tegan's grandfather had described to her in his letters. Everything about it was wrong. In her heart Tegan had known this would happen. 'Let's get out of here,' she cried.

Turlough agreed. One glance at the chaos out there had been enough to convince him that if they didn't move fast they would become part of the general disintegration. 'Quickly, Doctor,' he shouted. 'Relocate the TARDIS.'

But the Doctor had forestalled them. His arm was already moving towards the main control switch.

'No, wait!' As the dust cleared for a moment in the scanner frame Tegan saw something move. She couldn't be sure, but it seemed to her that there was a shifting among the shadows out there, that the grey hulk of a block of stone edged sideways. Instinctively she raised an arm to restrain her companions. 'Hold on, there's somebody out there!' she cried.

The others had seen it too, and were watching the screen closely. Suddenly the stone moved again and became an indistinct shadowy figure which rose up out of the dust and slipped away into the shadow of a pillar. It was bent nearly double, and it limped heavily, lurching over the rubble which littered the floor.

Another curtain of dust swept across the view.

'He's trapped,' the Doctor said anxiously. 'If there's another fall he'll be killed.' Before his companions realised what he was doing, he had reached across the console in front of Turlough, hit the slide control to open the main door of the TARDIS, and was on his way out.

Turlough gaped at the whirling dust filling the screen and blanched. 'We can't go out there!' he objected. A rescue mission would be suicidal – any fool could see that. But the Doctor was not at all interested in what fools could see, and Tegan was close behind him.

'Doctor!' Turlough complained. With a last helpless glance at the monitor and the now immobile time rotor, he gave a resigned shrug and hurried out after the others.

2

The Devil in the Church

Outside the TARDIS, the Doctor shone his torch into the gloom. The wandering beam picked out columns and archways. It soon became clear that they were inside a church crypt – one which was largely ruined already and was being further devastated every moment. Plaster and masonry crumbled and crashed to the floor with a noise that sped away into shadows, where it was swallowed up in the accumulated dust of centuries.

Frowning and straining her eyes in the poor light, Tegan searched for the figure they had seen on the scanner. To her right she distinguished two stone arches held up by decidedly rickety-looking pillars. If those went, the roof would cave in. Beyond the archways there ran a passage backed by a wall of tombs; these were rectangular holes in the wall blocked off with stones, on which crumbled, illegible lettering was just visible. There was no movement at all in that direction.

Ahead, across the crypt, two more arches on low columns led to a stone stairway. The steps veered up to the right and vanished out of sight; perhaps the man had gone up those. Or he might have lost himself among the black recesses to their left, where another decrepit archway gave on to deep, interminable shadow.

'He's gone,' she whispered. She shivered: it was cold in here, with the damp chill of old stone hidden deep in the earth, where sunlight had never been. She realised, too, how quiet everything had become: the falls of rubble

FIFE EDUCATIONAL
RESOURCES CENTRE

had ceased and their clattering had been replaced by a silence that was as heavy as lead. Tegan began to think she had imagined the man.

But the Doctor had seen him too. 'Hello!' he called, stepping away from the TARDIS and picking his way among the litter of collapsed stone.

'Hello!'

Now the recesses of the crypt soaked up his voice like a sponge, and the dusty darkness swallowed the thin beam of his torch. Turlough, at Tegan's shoulder, could see nothing at all, until suddenly one of the shadows beside the wall of tombs separated itself from a pillar. Moving incredibly fast, it limped silently up the side of the crypt and vanished again.

'Wait, please!' the Doctor shouted, setting off after it.

Tegan cried out with frustration: that brief glimpse had been enough to tell her that the man's clothes were all wrong for the twentieth century. They were more or less rags, but they most certainly were not twentieth-century rags – some kind of breeches and a shapeless woollen garment like a smock, which went over the man's head and shoulders, to be clutched around his throat.

She turned to Turlough in dismay. 'Did you see his clothes?' she wailed. 'We're in the wrong century!'

Turlough shook his head. 'We're not,' he assured her. 'I checked the time monitor. It *is* 1984.'

The Doctor shone his torch into Tegan's bewildered face. In a slightly mocking voice, sending up her disbelief, he said, 'Let's have a look around.' Without waiting for an answer he turned away and hurried across the crypt and ran up the stone steps out of sight.

Warily and apprehensively, Tegan and Turlough peered through the encircling gloom. The figure was nowhere to be seen. There seemed nothing to be gained from hanging around here waiting for the roof to fall in; they each glanced at the other for confirmation of

22

their thoughts, and ran after the Doctor as fast as they could.

When they, too, had vanished up the steps, the silence of centuries returned to the crypt. And noiselessly, as if he was part of that silence, the man appeared. Moving sideways like a ghostly crab, he slipped out of the cover of an archway and humped his aching body across the floor.

He reached the steps and craned his neck to look up the empty staircase. Although the dim light still did not reveal his features, it was strong enough to show that there was something wrong with his face.

Something terribly, sickeningly wrong.

The limping man would have fitted well into the parlour of Ben Wolsey's farmhouse. It too was far from modern: in fact, by deliberate design and through the painstaking collection of antique furnishings over the whole of his adult life, the big farmer had turned it into a place fit for history to repeat itself.

Friends and acquaintances who walked into the parlour felt immediately disoriented and lost, as if they had stepped through a time warp into the seventeenth century. Often the experience unnerved them, for every period detail was so exact that the room held the very smell and atmosphere of a bygone age.

When they had got over their initial surprise and looked for reasons for their superstitious reaction, some of Wolsey's acquaintances decided it was the heavy oak furniture which weighed so profoundly upon their spirits – the ornately carved chairs or the long table laden with maps and parchments and an ancient, forbidding, long-barrelled pistol. Others suspected the dark wood panelling on the walls, or the bulky drapes of curtains or the massive open stone fireplace.

For some, the silver candelabra on the mantelpiece

and the pot of spills and the displays of pewter plates conjured up, like ghosts, images of the people who once used them. And then there were those dark portraits of seventeenth-century country gentlefolk, and the huge hunting tapestry, and the collection of weapons from the English Civil War displayed ominously above the hearth. Perhaps it was those.

Whatever the reason, they all agreed that Wolsey had succeeded in creating something uncommonly exact – a room in which the dead days of long ago came back to life. One way or another it affected every person who entered it.

Jane Hampden, a schoolteacher who prided herself on being down-to-earth and practical, still found it eerie and unsettling. She found it to be a room which made her imagine things; sometimes she waited for seventeenth-century men to walk in through the door.

Today it actually happened.

She sat at the long table in front of the window, with a quill feather in her hands which was over three hundred and fifty years old, and looked at a Cavalier of King Charles the First standing at the fire, and a Colonel of Oliver Cromwell's army beside the door. It was uncanny. Jane felt her sense of reality take a jolt: for a moment she almost felt that it was she, in her twentieth-century clothes, who was the odd one out, an intruder from another age.

She felt uncomfortable, and more than ever before she experienced the strange sensation that this room actually held more than it appeared to contain – that these ancient trappings had brought with them something from their own century: overtones, associations, *memories*. It was that, she decided, which made the atmosphere in here so compelling.

Jane tried to pull herself together. It was ridiculous that a modern young schoolteacher should allow herself to think like that.

Sir George Hutchinson thought so too, and was telling her so in crystal clear terms. He stood in front of the fireplace, working that spongy black ball with his fingers, and adopted his most persuasive manner.

'I don't understand you,' he said. 'Every man, woman and child in this village is involved in the war game – except you. Why?' He tossed the ball and snatched it out of the air. 'It's great fun. An adventure.'

'I understand that,' Jane said. She tried to make her smile less mocking, but she still could not consider the prospect of an entire village raking up an old, unhappy, far-off war much fun.

Wolsey watched them both carefully, uncertain where he should stand in this difference of opinion. Neutrality seemed the safest option at the moment.

Sir George pursued his argument. 'Join us,' he invited Jane. 'Your influence may temper the more high-spirited, prevent accidents.'

'Look,' Jane explained, as if to one of her schoolchildren who had missed the point entirely, 'I don't care if a few high-spirited kids get their heads banged together. It's gone beyond that.' She looked at him sharply. 'Suppose what happened to me out there happens to someone else – a stranger, an innocent visitor to the village.'

Sir George leaned forward. 'There will be no visitors to the village,' he informed her. His voice was excited, his manner eager and intense – almost joyful – and his eyes shone. 'It has been isolated from the outside world. No-one can enter, or leave.'

He glanced triumphantly at Wolsey. The big man looked defiantly at Jane, who stared at both of them, appalled by this bland proposal. 'You can't do that!' she exploded.

Sir George stormed to the table, snatched up a map of the village and checked his lines of defence. 'Can't I?' he demanded. His voice was sharp now and he snapped the words, brooking no argument. 'It's been done.'

Persuasion time was over.

Yet even as Sir George spoke, across some fields outside the village, three strangers were climbing damp stone steps out of the ruined crypt of Little Hodcombe Church.

They emerged into a small side chapel. This led through an archway to the nave of the church. The Doctor was in front, as always eager for exploration; Tegan and Turlough were close behind him. All three, however, were stopped in their tracks by the sight which greeted their eyes when they entered the nave.

It was still a church, but only just: sunlight slanted through windows high in the walls and illuminated a scene of devastation. The Doctor and his companions looked across the nave at what seemed like the aftermath of some unspeakable carnage: dust and rubble were spread everywhere; roof timbers lay askew where they had fallen, among great blocks of stone; smashed pews had been tossed like sticks into corners.

And yet it was still most definitely an English country church. Two rows of pews remained standing; they faced a single, beautiful stained glass window in the end wall of the sanctuary. The stone pillars looked to be reasonably intact, and across from where they stood the companions could see a carved timber pulpit, seemingly unharmed, which might have been waiting for the village priest to enter and preach his sermon.

It was weird. The place was ruinous, silent and still, and it had obviously not been used for years . . . and yet, shabby and neglected though it was, it could be used, even now – it seemed to be waiting to be used. There was a feeling of anticipation. The Doctor, Tegan and Turlough all felt it.

They moved quickly forward, hoping to find the mysterious man from the crypt. The Doctor hurried across to the pulpit; Turlough marched down the nave, followed more slowly by Tegan, who looked around in wonder.

'Where did he go?' she asked.

'If he can move that quickly, he can't be hurt very badly,' Turlough said, looking back at her over his shoulder. He was unwilling to be here, and wanted very much to get back into the TARDIS and far away from this place, which was all too obviously in a state of collapse. Yet he felt its fascination, too. His annoyance was beginning to turn into a desire to find some answers to the questions which had been multiplying ever since they got here.

The Doctor, too, was fascinated. He crouched down beside the pulpit and ran his fingers over the sculpted wood. 'Interesting,' he muttered in such an enthralled tone that Tegan left off searching for the limping man and hurried over to have a look for herself.

What she saw made her shudder. Images were carved into the wooden side of the pulpit with such skill and twisted imagination that they made medieval gargoyles, of the kind she had seen on stone buttresses of old churches, look like fairies. There was a man being pursued around a tree by something monstrous . . . an inhuman, distorted and mask-like image that was utterly grotesque.

She shivered. 'I don't like it.'

'Then admire the craftsmanship,' the Doctor suggested, probing the carved relief with his fingers. 'It's seventeenth-century . . . probably on the theme of Man being chased by the Devil.' His finger hesitated beside the Devil. 'I must admit I've never seen one quite like that before.'

Turlough came over while the Doctor was speaking, but his attention was distracted by a crack in the church wall just below the pulpit – a horizontal split which suddenly veered upwards at its right extremity. The Doctor glanced across at it too, then put away his torch and gazed up at the vaulted roof for signs of damage there.

'It looks as though a bomb hit the place,' Tegan said, voicing a thought which had occurred to her earlier when they had first seen the cascading masonry on the scanner screen.

'Maybe it did,' Turlough agreed.

Tegan was suddenly anxious. 'Can we find my grandfather?' she pleaded. The Doctor nodded. He turned away from the cracked wall and waved her down the nave. With Turlough he followed Tegan between the dusty, rubble-laden pews. Then he heard the noise.

It was a single, short, hollow creak which whiplashed through the church like a gun going off. It was followed by complete silence.

'What was that?' Turlough shuddered.

'A ghost?' the Doctor suggested. He smiled at his joke but Tegan, far from being amused, was running. Suddenly she couldn't wait a moment longer to leave this strange place and get out into the everyday light of a sane, normal day, in her grandfather's village in twentieth-century England.

They left the church without turning back. If they had turned they might have seen that the creaking sound had been the audible sign of some kind of release, like a dam bursting inside the wall. Now a river of smoke was pouring down from the crack in the wall and seeping like a fog across the floor. And the crack itself was wider.

The Doctor and his companions came out of the church into the warm sunshine of a summer day. The light was so bright after the gloom inside that it dazzled their eyes. They were surrounded by the green grass of a churchyard. This in turn was encircled by a darker green of hedgerows and dotted with yew trees, in which unseen birds were singing. There was no time for Tegan or Turlough to appreciate their new situation, however,

28

because the Doctor was already striding along a gravel path towards an old-fashioned lych-gate, and they had to hurry to avoid being left behind. There was no sign of another building anywhere.

'Why did they build the church so far from the village?' Tegan wondered.

'Perhaps they were refused planning permission,' Turlough joked.

Everybody was trying to be funny today. But Tegan wasn't in the mood.

They caught up with the Doctor outside the lych gate, and found themselves on the threshold of a broad, undulating meadow. The Doctor had stopped, and was looking up a green hillside which stretched away to their left. He raised an arm to bring them to a halt.

'Behave yourselves,' he ordered. 'We have company.'

They followed his gaze and saw, etched sharply against the skyline where green hilltop met hard blue firmament, the dark, statuesque outline of a horseman. As they watched, he urged his horse into a canter and rode down the hillside in a line calculated to cut them off if they tried to cross the meadow.

Then they heard hooves beating behind them, too, and the harsh voices of men goading their horses. They turned and saw three more horsemen break cover behind the tree-fringed churchyard and come galloping through the grass towards them.

Tegan's eyebrows shot up in surprise: the horsemen wore the steel pointed helmets and the breastplates of troopers of the English Civil War. She was going to point out the absurdity of this, but Turlough sensed danger and shouted, 'We should go back!'

But before they could retreat, armed foot soldiers in full battledress appeared around a corner of the church and came running towards them from behind.

They were trapped. The Doctor spun round, frantically searching for an escape route, but all ways were

29

denied them, by mounted troopers looming close and now forcing them back against a hedge, and foot soldiers racing up the path to the lych gate. 'Too late,' he muttered. They could only face their attackers like cornered animals.

'Sergeant' Joseph Willow glared down at them through the steel bars of his visor, from the safe height of his big grey horse. 'Where do you think you're going?' he snarled. He had the rasping, ill-tempered voice of a natural bully. 'This is Sir George Hutchinson's land.'

The Doctor looked up at him. Instinctively aware of the man's short temper, he took a deep breath. This was a moment for patience and sweet reason, not anger. 'If we are trespassing,' he said mildly, 'I apologise.'

It was an apology which Willow refused to accept. 'Little Hodcombe,' he persisted, 'is a closed area, for your own safety. We're in the middle of a war game.'

Now Tegan understood their armour and weapons. These were grown men playing at historical soldiers – but even so, surely they were being too aggressive? The threat in their drawn swords was very real. 'We're here to visit my grandfather,' she explained, anxious like the Doctor to calm things down.

Willow didn't want her explanations either. 'You'd better see Sir George,' he said curtly. 'He'll sort it out.' He urged his horse forward, moving between them and the hedge. 'Move out!' he shouted.

At his command, the troopers and the foot soldiers closed in around the Doctor and his companions, forming a bizarre prisoners' escort. Then, led by Sergeant Willow, the party moved across the meadow towards Little Hodcombe village and Sir George Hutchinson.

As they went, there peered around a crumbling, mossy gravestone in the churchyard the head of the limping, beggar-like figure they had glimpsed briefly in the crypt. As he watched the strangers being led away, the sun illuminated his devastated face.

His left eye was gone. Where it should have been, wrinkled skin collapsed into a shrivelled, empty socket. The man's mouth twisted awkwardly towards this, and the entire left side of his face was dead. It looked as if it had been burned once, long ago, as if the skin had been blasted by fire and transformed into a hard, waxen shell which now could feel no pain – or any other sensation.

Holding the coarse woollen cloth around his throat, so that it hooded his head, he knelt behind a gravestone and stared, with his one unblinking eye, at the Doctor, Tegan and Turlough being herded away through the grass.

After an undignified forced march, at first among fields and then between the scattered cottages and farmsteads of Little Hodcombe, the Doctor and his companions were escorted to a big, rambling farmhouse next to an almost enclosed yard. Here Willow and the troopers dismounted and at sword and pistol point forced the trio inside, then pushed them into a room that was straight out of another century.

The Doctor, who was first to enter, could not disguise his surprise at the sight of this antique room and the burly, red-faced man in Parliamentary battle uniform who sat on a carved oak settle, facing him. For a second he wondered, as Tegan had done, whether somehow all their instruments had gone wrong and they had turned up hundreds of years awry, but then he saw Jane Hampden sitting at a table by the window in casual, twentieth-century clothes. Reassured by that, he tried to relax, yet still he felt uncertain; all these efforts to make the twentieth century seem like the seventeenth were unsettling.

The sight of three strangers being thrust unceremoniously into his parlour caused Ben Wolsey to jump out

31

of his seat in surprise. 'What's going on here?' he demanded.

Willow followed them inside and closed the door. His hand hovered on the hilt of his sword. 'They're trespassers, Colonel,' he answered curtly. 'I've arrested them.'

Willow's final shove had sent Tegan and Turlough staggering across the room towards a small woman, who sat at a long oak table with outrage and astonishment spreading across her face. 'I don't believe this!' she exploded, and jumped to her feet.

Wolsey's face, too, was a picture of surprise and embarrassment. 'Are you sure you should be doing this?' he challenged Willow.

The Sergeant casually removed his riding gloves. 'Sir George has been informed,' was all he would say in reply.

Wolsey turned to the Doctor with an apologetic smile. 'I'm sorry about this,' he said. 'Some of the men get a bit carried away. We'll soon have this business sorted out and you safely on your way.'

The Doctor, who had been giving the room a close examination, now turned to Wolsey. He leaned forward and treated the farmer to his most courteous smile. 'Thank you,' he said, with only the slightest hint of sarcasm. Indicating the furnishings, he added, 'This is a very impressive room, Colonel.'

Ben Wolsey smiled proudly. His head nodded with pleasure at approval from a stranger. 'It's my pride and joy,' he confided.

'Seventeenth century?'

'Yes,' Wolsey nodded again. 'And it's perfect in every detail.'

Tegan felt exasperated: chatting about antiques wasn't going to get them very far. Beginning to think they had entered a lunatic asylum, she glared at the woman who, because she was wearing normal clothes, seemed to Tegan to be the only sane person around here. 'What is going on?' she asked her.

Jane smiled and shrugged her shoulders. 'I'm sorry, but I just don't know,' she admitted. 'I think everyone's gone mad.'

That made two of them. 'Look,' Tegan tried to sound more reasonable than she felt, 'we don't want to interfere. We're just here to visit my grandfather.'

'Oh yes, so you said,' the Sergeant snapped, barging into their conversation as he had barged into their lives. 'And who might he be?'

'His name is Andrew Verney.'

Just two simple words – a name – but their effect was enormous. A stunned silence followed, and the atmosphere became electric. Tegan felt almost physically the shock her words had inflicted upon these villagers. She saw their hasty glances at each other and noticed Joseph Willow look for instructions from the big Roundhead soldier he called Colonel.

'Verney?' he prodded, but the red-faced man said nothing; he appeared to be embarrassed, and not to know what to say. Tegan felt suddenly apprehensive.

'What's wrong?' she demanded.

Jane Hampden was also looking to Ben Wolsey for some explanation, but he remained stolidly silent and eventually she herself turned to Tegan. As gently as she could, she said, 'He disappeared a few days ago.'

Tegan's apprehension became chilling anxiety. 'Has anything been done to find him?'

'Ben?' Again Jane turned to Ben Wolsey, and again the farmer refused to answer, dropping his eyes and turning away.

'Well?' Tegan shouted.

It was time for the Doctor to act: he knew the signs and was only too well aware of Tegan's talent for jumping to conclusions and diving in at the deep end of things. He walked quickly towards her and held up his hands for restraint. 'Now calm down, Tegan,' he warned. 'I'm sure we can sort this out.'

But Tegan was in the grip of her anxiety and in no mood for more talk. With a frustrated cry of 'Oh, for heaven's sake!' at the prevaricating fools around her, she made a dash for the door and was through it before anyone else even moved.

The Doctor was the first to react. He called, 'Now Tegan, come back!' – but even as the words rang out he knew it was useless, and in the same instant he turned to his other companion and shouted, 'Turlough! Fetch her, would you? Please?'

Turlough reacted quickly this time. He was fast on his feet and had hurled himself through the door before Willow's hand reached the pistol on the table.

But now Willow snatched it up and pointed the barrel right between the Doctor's eyes, in case he should have any thought of following his young friends. 'You!' he screamed, 'Stay where you are!' He was furious with himself for allowing the escape; anger twitched the skin of his cheek, and his finger hovered dangerously over the trigger.

The Doctor looked into the round, ominous tube of the barrel, and raised his hands in surrender.

3

The Body in the Barn

Tegan ran blindly out of the farmhouse into dazzling sunlight. Propelled by fear for her grandfather's safety, and bewildered that such events could be happening in a supposedly peaceful English village, she didn't care where she was going so long as she got away from Willow and the troopers. She could make some firm plans later. So now, clutching her scarlet handbag, she stumbled over the uneven farmyard and raced towards the shelter of some buildings on the other side, hoping to reach them before anyone came out of the house to see which way she had gone.

She dived around the corner of a barn, and stopped. She was gasping for breath and leaned against the barn wall for support, beside its open doorway. The bricks, warmed by the sun, burned against her back.

Tegan pressed the handbag against her forehead to feel its coolness, but no sooner had she done so than it was roughly snatched out of her fingers, and with a shock she saw a hand disappear with it into the barn.

She thrust herself off the wall and into the doorway, but the deep shadow inside made her pause. It looked solid as a wall, black and still – she could see nothing in there. 'What are you doing?' she shouted. The shadows soaked up her voice like blotting paper. 'Give me that back!' she called again.

Taking a deep breath, she stepped forward into the velvet darkness. It wrapped itself around her like a cloak.

After the glare outside it took a moment or two for Tegan's eyes to grow accustomed to the gloom. Then she saw a floor stretching away into even deeper shadow, littered with farm produce, implements, sacks and bales of hay. A rope hung from a hook on the wall and a rickety wooden staircase led up to a dark gallery above.

Everything was still. There was no sound, and no sign of the person who had snatched her handbag. He had simply disappeared. Unless. . . Tegan approached the stairs. The thief might be above her head at this moment, crouching up there in the dark gallery, waiting quietly for her to give up. But Tegan was not about to give up – she decided she had been pushed around enough for one day.

It was a basic fact of Tegan's nature that her emotions sometimes drove her to take risks. That was part of her courage. Now her frustration and anger were coming to a dangerous head and she was quite prepared to venture where others would fear to tread: with a glance at the inky blackness above, and knowing full well that there was probably something nasty up there waiting for her, she began to climb the steps.

But when she was only part way up the staircase the big door of the barn slammed shut with a bang like a cannon going off. Now she was enclosed in total darkness. The noise set her nerves tingling, and now that the light from the doorway had been cut off she felt a sensation of claustrophobia so choking that she was forced to turn and hurry back down the steps towards the door.

She felt as if the barn, like those great dark beasts in nightmares, had opened its arms to envelop her. She had to get out fast, or be swallowed up.

In his Cavalier clothes Sir George Hutchinson looked like a brilliantly plumed bird as he swept into Ben Wolsey's parlour. What he saw – his Sergeant pointing a pistol into the eyes of a stranger – displeased him, for it implied unlooked-for complications when there were already enough matters of overwhelming importance to be dealt with.

'What's this?' he growled.

Without taking his eyes from the Doctor, Willow explained, 'He tried to escape, sir.'

With a gesture of impatience Sir George pushed down Willow's arm. 'But he isn't a prisoner, Sergeant Willow.' He kept his voice mild and friendly, for the stranger's benefit. 'You must treat visitors with more respect.'

Surprised by his Commander's attitude, Willow lowered the pistol. Sir George smiled placatingly at the Doctor, then turned away to glance at Wolsey and find somewhere to lay his hat. The Doctor, no longer under immediate threat, felt encouraged to speak to the new arrival: Sir George was only too obviously involved in these War Games, and he also seemed to be in control around here.

'What is going on?' he demanded, like Sir George keeping as civil a tone as he could manage.

Sir George spun round. His eyes glowed. 'A celebration!' he cried. His expression displayed pleasure and triumph and his voice an eager, tense excitement. He moved close to the Doctor, almost alight with anticipation, like a firework about to go off. 'On the thirteenth of July, sixteen hundred and forty three,' he exclaimed, 'the English Civil War came to Little Hodcombe. A Parliamentary force and a regiment for the King destroyed each other – and the village.'

He made it sound like a party. 'And you're celebrating *that*?' the Doctor asked, puzzled by this feverish excitement.

'And why not?' Sir George's words were thrown down like a challenge; as he removed his riding gloves he watched the Doctor closely for a reaction. 'It's our heritage,' he continued.

'It's a madness,' Jane exclaimed, unable to contain her impatience with such talk any longer.

Hutchinson treated her to a sardonic, dismissive smile. 'Miss Hampden disagrees with our activities.'

'I can understand why,' the Doctor said, looking at the sadistic enjoyment on Willow's face.

Irritated by their opposition, Sir George held out a chair for Jane, inviting her to sit down and keep quiet. Then, moving around the table to approach the Doctor, he looked him up and down and demanded, in a voice clipped with anger, 'Who are you?'

'I'm known as the Doctor.' The Doctor blandly endured Sir George's examination, aware of his puzzlement at the frock coat, cricket pullover and sprig of celery in his buttonhole.

'Are you a member of the theatrical profession?' Sir George finally asked.

The Doctor smiled. 'No more than you are.'

'Aha!' Sir George laughed at the joke, but his sideways glance at Wolsey was humourless, hinting that these intruders might turn out to be more of a nuisance than at first appeared. Then he glared sharply into the Doctor's eyes. 'How did you get to the village?'

'Through the woods, via the church,' the Doctor bluffed.

'That's where I found him, sir,' Willow confirmed.

Sir George was silent for a moment. He studied his gloves, flicking them against his hand. When he spoke again his voice was quiet and deliberate, and contained more than a hint of threat. 'I would avoid the church if I were you,' he said. 'It's very dangerous. It could fall down at any minute.'

'So I noticed.'

'However,' Sir George smiled, now deliberately lightening the tone of their conversation, 'since you're here you must join in our game. It's our final battle.'

'Do you know, I'd love to,' the Doctor replied, equally

38

amiably. His relaxed voice disguised a rapidly increasing nervous tension, for he was gearing himself for action. 'But first I must find Tegan and Turlough. And Tegan's grandfather – I gather he's disappeared. Good day,' he concluded, and with a single movement of his arm swept maps, papers and pistol from the table before turning on his heel and running for the door.

The lightness of his tone had fooled the others completely and this sudden explosion of activity took them all by surprise. All Sir George could do was shout, 'Wait! Wait!' and by the time Willow had dived for the pistol and levelled it at the doorway, the Doctor had gone.

'Wait!' Sir George shouted for a third time. But he knew he was wasting his breath, and when Willow turned to him and told him that Tegan was Verney's grand-daughter, his face set into stone. All the affected bonhomie with which he had addressed the Doctor vanished completely.

'Double the perimeter guard,' he snapped. 'He mustn't get out of the village.' Then a new thought struck him and his smile returned. 'And help him find Verney's grand-daughter . . .'

'Right!' Willow snapped his heels together.

'I've something rather special in mind for her,' Sir George grinned. The look of eager anticipation on Willow's face showed that he fully understood all the implications of that remark.

Sir George turned to Jane. She had watched these proceedings with increasing concern and now registered her disapproval again: 'Detaining people against their will is illegal, Sir George. The Doctor and his friends included.'

Hutchinson leaned down over the table towards her. 'I shouldn't let that bother you, Miss Hampden,' he sneered. 'As the local magistrate, I shall find myself quite innocent.' There was something so abnormal about the intense brilliance in his eyes, and so sardonic in his complacent half-smile, that Jane shuddered. For a moment she felt physically sick. This man held all the aces. There was no stopping him.

The barn door was immovable. Tegan pushed and pulled and grunted; she kicked it and bruised her toes, and stretched up to wrench at a padlock high on the door until her nails split, but it would not open. When it had slammed shut, it had jammed tight.

Panting with the effort, she gave up the struggle. She needed to rest for a moment, and toppled forward to lean her head against the door. The wood smelled of old age and creosote and pitch. She gasped for breath, thankful at least that the thief who had stolen her handbag was not shut in here with her, in the darkness. He had simply disappeared – it was probably he who had slammed the door shut on her, on his way out.

But even as she breathed that sigh of relief she felt that there was *something* in here. Something odd.

As she leaned with her forehead pressed against the musty wood, she heard a strange, unidentifiable sound. It was not a single note, but a continuing long, low hum which grew louder and stronger and gradually became a pressure which hurt her ears. She stiffened. There was a tingling sensation in her spine and she felt a sudden apprehension that something weird was building up in the gloom behind her.

She hardly dared to look round. But when she did she breathed another sigh of relief, for there was nothing to be seen. There was just the whirring sound in the darkness. But then – she stiffened again – she saw something in the gloom up above her, where she had supposed the gallery to be. She strained her eyes to see, and suddenly discovered a light dancing around up there in the dark.

Now the noise in Tegan's ears began to change in pitch. It rose and crescendoed and abruptly shattered like glass, breaking into tinkling fragments of sound that sparkled like droplets in the still air of the barn. At the same time the light became more and more brilliant, and then it too broke, dividing and dividing over and over until there was a constantly changing kaleidoscope of points of light up there. They whirled below the invisible rafters, now spreading, now contracting, accompanied always by the tinkling noise.

Backed up against the door, Tegan stared upwards at these flickering movements that were both light and sound together. They fascinated and frightened her at the same time, and she felt her body begin to tremble so violently that she had to press into the rough timber to steady herself. Then she gasped: something was happening *inside* the lights.

Between the pinpoints of brilliance ceaselessly dancing and vibrating a glow began to emerge – still, solid and white, it was spreading and forming into a kind of shape . . .

Tegan felt a scream rise in her throat as the glow steadied into the distinct shape of the torso of a man – a pale, grey-white, headless body suspended up there in the darkness under the roof. Ribs protruded from its gaunt, naked chest; two arms hung bare and limp at the sides and folds of sacking were loosely draped about its waist. Its skin was as pallid as the skin of a corpse.

The noise had changed once more, dropping again to a deep hum that seemed to surround the glowing torso like a force holding it together. The lights which still played about it moved less violently now. But suddenly everything activated again: the lights whirled and leaped about and the droplets of sound sparkled. The torso faded from sight. It was replaced by a disembodied head.

'Oh no,' Tegan whimpered. She pressed back against the door, as if she was trying to burrow down inside it.

It was the head of a very old man, and it stared down at her with cold, dead eyes. Long white hair drooped

41

lankly about a pallid, sad, tired-looking face, whose skin seemed all wrinkled up, folded and waxen and dead as paper.

The face looked down at her. Tegan was sure it was looking at her. 'Oh, no!' she shrieked, for this was more than real flesh and blood could stand. She hammered on the heavy door. 'Come on!' she yelled at it as the lights flashed above her and the humming sound returned and swelled loud enough to burst her ears.

Desperately she looked back. The face was growing larger by the second. And it was moving . . . forward and down, swooping towards her and looming now just above her head. She shrieked again and pushed and pounded the door, and suddenly it moved.

But it moved the wrong way. It was moving an impossible way, inwards, against the force of her pushing, thrust by an outside agency that was stronger than she was. Her breath gagged in her throat; the door jerked and swung inwards and swept her off her feet.

Tegan rolled across the floor among rotting vegetables and sacking and straw, and saw the door swing wide open. Sunlight flooded through, and then a shadow fell across her and a hand gripped her shoulder; she screamed again as a figure leaned down and another face swooped and loomed down low above hers.

'Oh! It's you!' It was Turlough's face. Relief surged through Tegan as he took her arm and helped her to her feet.

'What's happening?' Turlough asked, puzzled to see her so distraught.

Tegan could not stop trembling. Nervously she looked around the barn and up towards the gallery. She saw nothing – there was nothing there to see now. There were no lights, no sounds, no torso or dead, staring face. How could she possibly explain to Turlough?

'Later,' she muttered. 'Let's get away from here first.'

And to Turlough's astonishment she ran from the barn as though a ghost was after her.

It was blazing hot in the streets of the village. The sun flared out of a hard blue sky as the Doctor hurried about the roads and lanes in search of Tegan and Turlough. He was surprised at the lack of human life anywhere. The place seemed deserted; there was neither movement nor any noise, other than the constant barrage of birdsong which seemed to surround the village like an invisible sound barrier.

It felt as though the shimmering heat had taken all living things into suspension and the whole village was holding its breath, waiting for something to happen. The Doctor felt this atmosphere of suspense keenly, and he was getting worried. He had looked everywhere in the village: up and down side streets and alleyways, running across gardens bright with flowers and past scattered, white-painted cottages, some of them thatched, and barns with red-tiled roofs and stone walls.

Every building cast a hard black shadow across the grass verges that had burned brown during weeks of drought. The Doctor had searched among the shadows and in the sunlight, and had found no sign at all of his companions.

Now, crossing another deserted street, he turned to look back the way he had come. 'Turlough! Tegan!' he called again. A moment later he was lying in the road.

The beggarman had seemed to come from nowhere. He was just there, suddenly looming out of a roadside shadow straight at the Doctor and catching him off balance with a shoulder charge that sent him sprawling. As he fell, the Doctor saw him lurch away up the street with the rolling, limping gait of the figure they had seen in the crypt; the man clutched some sort of coarsely woven cloth about his head and shoulders, and there was something terribly wrong with his face. The Doctor

43

winced: it looked like a stricken landscape in the after-math of an explosion.

But what made the Doctor really catch his breath was the sight of Tegan's handbag held tightly against the man's chest as he ran. He pulled himself to his feet and shouted, 'Wait! Come back!'

The man turned sideways, out of the street into a lane. Sprinting his fastest, the Doctor was at the spot within seconds, yet what he saw was an empty lane, stretching away between high walls. It led far into the distance, green and deserted except for a tiny, black, diminishing figure almost at the horizon. The figure was going like the wind.

For a moment the Doctor doubted the evidence of his own eyes. 'How could he get so far?' he muttered, and set off running again.

While the Doctor was chasing the half-blind, limping beggar, another part of Little Hodcombe was stirring from its lethargy.

Four horsemen were approaching the village Cross, a worn stone Celtic monument set upon a hexagonal plinth at a spot where four roadways converged. Here, village and countryside met together in a conglomeration of thatched houses, orchards, and a telephone box, stone and asphalt and trees and grass all wilting under the unyielding sun.

Ben Wolsey, Joseph Willow and the two troopers who cantered behind them sweated inside their Civil War battledress. They too were searching for Tegan and, like the Doctor, they were having no success at all.

When they arrived at the telephone box Wolsey reined his big grey horse to a halt and looked about him in frustration. 'We'll never find her,' he exclaimed. 'She could be anywhere.'

Willow cantered back. 'We should ask for more men,' he said.

'Hutchinson won't allow it. He's got everyone guarding the perimeter.'

Willow frowned. In a voice hard-edged with anger he shouted, 'We're wasting our time with only four of us searching. If he wants her so badly, he's got to find more men!'

Wolsey pointed to the telephone box. The paint gleamed as scarlet as blood in the glaring light. 'Ring him,' he suggested.

Willow shook his head and wheeled his horse around, ready to set off again. 'We're not allowed. I'll have to go back to the house.'

'All right,' Wolsey agreed. He turned to the two troopers, who had also stopped and were patiently waiting for instructions. 'Carry on searching, you two,' he ordered them. 'Try Verney's cottage again. She might be there.'

With a noisy clatter of sparking hooves on the hard surface of the roadway, the troopers galloped away. Wolsey turned back to Willow. 'I'll come with you,' he said.

Wearily they set off again, in the direction of Wolsey's farmhouse.

Very warily, the Doctor entered the church. He was still in pursuit of the limping man and was sure he had run into the church – although somehow being sure no longer seemed sufficient reason to believe things in Little Hodcombe, because hardly anything was as it appeared to be at first sight.

That had happened again now: although he would have sworn that the man was in here, there was no sign of him. The Doctor came straight into the nave through a door in the back wall, behind the rubble-strewn pews; the nave stretched out before him, quiet and still and empty.

'Hallo!' he called. The sound echoed among the

45

pillared archways and sped to the sanctuary and the high, stained glass window at the other end of the church, facing him. 'I saw you enter,' he called again, but he might as well have been talking to himself.

Something in here tickled his throat and made him want to cough. He looked around, and sniffed. There was a strangely acrid smell which hadn't been here earlier. It mingled with the scents of rubble and damp and centuries of dust. He sniffed again, trying to identify it.

'All I want is Tegan's bag!' he shouted. 'What have you done with her? I know you can hear me!' Again his voice echoed and died, and the place was silent as a grave once more.

No, it wasn't.

For a moment the Doctor thought his ears were deceiving him, as out of the silence there grew, softly at first, a strange amalgamation of sounds without apparent cause. There was a trumpet, he decided ... no, there was more than one, there were several trumpets calling, and there were drums beating softly, and other noises, all of them low and far away.

Curious to identify their source, the Doctor walked carefully up the nave. The sounds seemed to be louder here, and they were growing louder by the moment as if they were coming closer. Now he could hear harness jingling, and horses neighing and whinnying, and the beat of their galloping hooves; and men were shouting and cursing. He sniffed ... that smell was stronger now – and suddenly he knew what it was.

'Gunpowder!' he hissed. Worried, he looked for traces of smoke, and noticed a thin white trail worming out of the crack in the wall, which seemed to be larger now than before. Whether that was the cause or not, gunpowder spoke to the Doctor of violence, and so did the noises. These were becoming very violent indeed: guns fired, cannon pounded, swords clashed. The nave reverberated with the uproar, and it began to vibrate inside the Doctor's head.

Trumpets, guns, harness, drums, shouting – the yelling and screaming of men in mortal agony – all the clamour of a desperate battle assailed the Doctor's ears. They raced around the church and echoed back and beat his senses like physical blows, and became a hurricane of noise that roared around and blew down across him until he buckled under the weight of it, his knees bending and his face twisting with pain.

The Doctor jammed his hands over his ears. The pressure made him cry out, and his cry was added to the rest and it too distorted and echoed and swelled and boomeranged back at him. The plunging sounds destroyed his balance, and he could no longer stand upright. He reeled, and spun round and round in the severest pain.

Finally he managed to stagger into a pew beside the pulpit. He half sat, half lay there, holding his ears. And the wall next to the pulpit, beside his head, split asunder.

The noise was like a pistol shot. It cracked through the Doctor's inner ear and killed every other sound. Not far from his face, the plaster on the wall bucked outwards. In astonishment the Doctor watched it widen to a hole, watched masonry come tumbling and dust fly as the wall was punched and harried and pulverised by something forcing its way out from the inside.

Suddenly the Doctor realised that the other racket had stopped altogether; the reverberations of battle had died away as mysteriously as they had risen. Everything in the church was still and silent again, and there was a tense atmosphere, as if all attention was focussed on this bulging and breaking of the wall. The Doctor gasped as something probed jerkily through the spreading gap towards him.

Fingers.

Fingers pushing and scraping and bleeding, yanking

47

at the wall and tearing out the plaster with feverish, desperate movements. Suddenly the fingers became a hand, and then the hand was clear of the hole and an arm followed, and then a shoulder was through, and all at once the wall gave way with a clatter, and a body burst out of it in a shower of plaster and dust.

4

Of Psychic Things

Utterly perplexed by this development, the Doctor simply gaped as the limbs bursting out of the wall finally became still. A youth stood beside him, coughing and spluttering and beating dust out of his clothes.

These were genuine seventeenth-century garments – a loose leather jerkin that had seen much better days, a shirt of coarse grey homespun cloth, ragged trousers and heavy buckled shoes. The body inside them was short and stocky, topped by a round moon face wearing a truculent expression. He was filthy dirty. His fingers bled from their efforts at battering masonry and the light dazzled his eyes. He rocked on his heels, spitting grime from his mouth, and looked belligerently about him.

When his eyes focussed on the astonished Doctor, they opened wide in surprise. 'What took 'ee zo long?' he demanded, in a thick, antiquated burr. 'I bin in thur for ages!' Then he noticed the Doctor's clothes, and his voice trailed away in awe.

Now the Doctor found his voice. 'Who are you?' he asked, giving what he hoped was a reassuring smile. Evidently it wasn't, because the youth retreated with a worried and uncertain look on his face. The Doctor offered him an even more confident smile, and held out his hand. 'I'm the Doctor,' he said.

The youth withdrew some more. He backed right away from the Doctor's hand. 'Doctor?' he asked. 'Doctor bain't a proper name.' Then he cocked his head on one side and said in a proud voice, 'Will Chandler be a proper name.'

Encouraged, the Doctor moved towards him. The effect was an immediate return to belligerence: startled and aggressive, the youth stooped and picked up a stone to defend himself. He had his back against the wall, and could go no further.

'Get 'ee off me,' he demanded.

'I won't hurt you.'

'I won't let 'ee.'

The Doctor paused. He regarded this Will Chandler very carefully, and with some uncertainty. After all, he reflected, it isn't every day that you see somebody come out of a wall. His mind raced, forming theories and as readily discarding them. There was one idea, however, which would not go away; it steadily gained conviction in the Doctor's mind, even though he knew it was impossible.

Suddenly Will Chandler's aggression left him; he winced and held his right hand tenderly. 'My hand's hurtin',' he muttered, all at once feeling sorry for himself.

The Doctor held out his left hand. 'Show me,' he said firmly.

Tentatively, Will raised his arm. The Doctor took hold of it gently and felt it all over, not just for breaks or other injuries but to confirm for himself that this youth was actually *real*. The arm was solid enough, and warm, and the flesh yielded under his fingers. Apart from grazing and bruising, it was intact.

The Doctor nodded towards the shattered wall. 'What were you doing in there?'

'It's a priest hole, ain't it?' Will said truculently. 'I hid from fightin'.'

The Doctor frowned. 'What fighting?'

The question revealed ignorance of large proportions, seemingly, or even stupidity, for Will's face puckered up

50

into a disbelieving smile and he withdrew his arm from the Doctor's hand.

'What fightin'? Ho, wur you been, then?' There was genuine puzzlement in his voice.

The Doctor felt that his idea was gaining ground, and credulity. Casually he put his hands into his pockets, then leaned down towards Will's face. 'What year is it?' he asked him.

Will reacted with a broad grin. 'I knows that un,' he said in a pleased voice, as if he was answering a teacher's question in school. But despite his confidence he hesitated, walking around the Doctor and getting his brain into gear, making sure he got this right. 'Year's . . . zixteen hunnerd an' forty . . . three!' He finished with a triumphant flourish, but his hand was hurting again and he sat down in a pew and nursed it, grunting with the pain.

'Sixteen hundred and forty three, eh?' The Doctor looked at Will Chandler with much sympathy but, as yet, not a lot of understanding. His idea had been valid, after all. He was not really surprised, for each of the events which had piled one on top of the other since they arrived in Little Hodcombe seemed stranger and more inexplicable than the last. This one, though, was a real puzzle; what was happening in Little Hodcombe was turning out to be much more complex and intriguing than the Doctor had first surmised.

Struck by a sudden thought, Will gave the Doctor an apprehensive look. 'Is battle done?' he asked. His voice shaking; he sat back and waited for the answer, terrified of what it might be.

'Yes,' the Doctor answered gently, reassuring him and wiping away his dread. 'Yes, Will. Battle's done.'

But the calming effect of his words was shattered by the door being thrown open wide with a bang that echoed the length and breadth of the church. Whimpering with fright, Will dived behind a pew as Tegan and Turlough came tumbling up the nave.

They were so out of breath with running that when they reached the Doctor they could hardly speak. The Doctor, delighted to see them both safe and well, looked at Will Chandler out of the corner of his eye and said cryptically, 'You're just in time.'

Misunderstanding him, Tegan cried out in frustration, 'Just in time? We almost didn't make it!'

'We have to get out of here!' Turlough's chest was heaving for breath, and his voice betrayed the stress he was suffering.

Recalling the incident in the barn made Tegan shudder: how could she put that into words? 'There's something very strange going on,' she said simply.

The Doctor, however, seemed to understand without the need for words. 'Yes, I know,' he said sympathetically.

At that moment, out of the corner of his eye Turlough saw Will peeping at them over the top of a pew. 'Who is that?' he asked, in a tone which betrayed extreme distaste at the sight of that grubby urchin face.

Tegan looked, saw Will's clothes and drew in her breath sharply, but refrained from comment. The Doctor merely smiled at Will. 'Will Chandler?' he asked, for confirmation. Will nodded, without taking his eyes off Tegan and Turlough.

'Where did he come from?' Tegan asked.

'Ah, well,' the Doctor said laconically. He smiled and shrugged. 'That's something we're going to have to talk about . . .'

In the seventeenth-century parlour of Ben Wolsey's farmhouse, Sir George Hutchinson, country squire and, while the War Game lasted, Cavalier General Extraordinary, stood in front of the fire and casually played with the spongy, black, metallically-shining ball. He kept kneading it in his fingers and examining it with never-ending fascination.

From her position beside the window, Jane watched him with growing anger. She was about to have another go at his complacent arrogance when raised voices and heavy footsteps in the next room announced the arrival of Ben Wolsey and Joseph Willow.

As soon as the door opened and they marched in, Sir George turned to them eagerly. 'Where is she?' he demanded.

Wolsey raised his visor. 'We can't find her,' he admitted. 'We'll need more men.'

Sir George was furious. With reddening face and narrowed eyes, his manner was suddenly extremely threatening, even towards the big farmer. He snapped, 'I want Tegan, not excuses, Wolsey.'

Ben Wolsey, taken aback, frowned with surprise at his tone. Jane was incensed. 'Don't listen to him, Ben,' she cried.

Sir George turned to her now. His eyes blazed and it was Jane's turn to be shocked by the vehemence of his manner and the anger behind his words. 'Miss Hampden! You're beginning to bore me with your constant bleating!' His attitude was contemptuous in the extreme. He stood there in his finery and glared at her, his hand ceaselessly working at the silver-sheened substance; for a moment Jane thought he was going to throw it at her.

The Sergeant intervened to support his General. 'She doesn't understand,' Willow leered. 'We must have our Queen of the May.'

Queen of the May! Jane winced. Andrew Verney had told her once how Little Hodcombe used to treat its May Queen. The story came back to her, and the picture his words had conjured up in her imagination returned with it. It had made her feel sick then, and it made her tremble now. As if to reinforce her fears, Sir George fairly shouted, 'Precisely!' He looked at her with a gleaming

53

smile and said, 'Think of it as a resurrection of an old tradition.'

Jane felt sick again. 'I know the way you plan to celebrate it,' she cried. 'I know the custom of this village. I know what happens to a May Queen at the end of her reign!'

Ben Wolsey looked genuinely surprised. His gentle, ruddy, farmer's face was as innocent as a baby's. 'We're not going to harm her,' he protested.

Jane shook her head. '*You* might not, Ben. I'm not so sure about them.'

Sir George closed the subject. He brought the conversation to an abrupt end by marching to the table and snatching up his riding gloves. 'The tradition must continue,' he said, in a tone that was quiet, authoritative and brooked no opposition. It held something very like awe – even reverence – as he looked from one to the other of them and said, 'Something is coming to our village. Something very wonderful, and strange.'

Then he cleared a path for himself between Wolsey and Willow and left the room. They watched him go, Cavalier and Roundhead in an all too serious War Game. Sir George's last remark hung cryptically in the air.

Wolsey, puzzled, said, 'We must find Tegan,' and made for the door.

'You're so gullible, Ben,' Jane shouted. 'You do anything he says!' If she had hoped that would stop him, she was disappointed. Wolsey ignored her, and went out without a word.

Willow was left alone at last with this nuisance of a schoolteacher, who was using every possible opportunity to try to spoil the fun. Uneasily Jane saw how his lips tightened now, and the deliberate way he took off his gloves. As he looked at her, his irritation changed to fury.

Jane saw it happen. She saw the cloud move across his eyes and felt fear tingle the small of her back. Joseph

54

Willow was a man on a short fuse, and the fuse was already burning. 'Something is coming to our village,' Sir George had said, but so far as Jane was concerned it was already here, and showing in Willow's face – a kind of madness.

Suddenly she wanted to get away from him. 'Right,' she said, marching towards the door. 'I'm going to the police. I'll soon put a stop to this.'

But Willow thrust himself between her and the door. Roughly he pushed her away. 'Shut up!' he shouted as she staggered backwards. 'Just be grateful it's the stranger who is to be Queen of the May – it so easily could have been you!'

Jane recovered her balance and with all her strength slapped his face. Willow's cheeks reddened. His eyes filled with hatred. For a moment Jane thought he was going to strike her back, but instead he smiled, a cold smile that was laden with threat. 'It still might be you,' he said, 'if we don't find her.'

And with a triumphant smirk Joseph Willow, iron-shirted Sergeant-at-arms to General Sir George Hutchinson, turned on his heel and left the room. He slammed the door shut behind him.

Before Jane could follow, she heard a bolt being drawn and a key turned in the lock. Willow had made her a prisoner.

'There's been a confusion in time. Somehow, 1984 has become linked with 1643.'

Sitting in a pew in the church, crouched forward eagerly with his feet on the back of the pew in front of him, the Doctor was thinking out loud. His mind raced as he focussed his thoughts on Will Chandler's mysterious appearance and all the other strange events which had showered on them since their arrival in Little Hodcombe. He was drawing on all his vast store of knowledge and experience – and still coming up with blanks.

55

Tegan and Turlough, now recovered from their flight, sat in the pews too and waited for the Doctor to come up with some answers. Will Chandler lay flat out at the Doctor's side; exhausted by his experience and bewildered by the Doctor's theories, he had taken refuge in unconsciousness and sprawled on the unyielding seat, fast asleep.

Turlough looked at him, and considered the Doctor's theory. A confusion in time? That left half the problems unanswered. 'What about the apparitions?' he asked.

The Doctor looked at him closely, watching for his reaction to the next part of his theory. 'Psychic projections,' he said.

Tegan drew in her breath. She wasn't keen on that. It was a spooky idea and she preferred rational, practical explanations. But after her experience in the barn, and with twentieth-century men pretending they were in the seventeenth century, and seventeenth-century youths suddenly appearing in the twentieth century, it was no wonder the Doctor called time 'confused'. It wasn't the only one, she reflected. Yet she shuddered at the possibility which the Doctor was suggesting, and tried to find a hole in the argument. 'What about the man we saw when we arrived?' she protested. 'He was real enough.'

'He was still a psychic projection,' the Doctor insisted. 'But with substance.'

Tegan frowned. Talking of psychic things was getting close to talking about ghosts, and nothing in that line would really surprise her now, after what she had seen.

Turlough grew more enthusiastic the more he considered the idea. He got up and wandered about, trying to absorb the implications and coming to terms with them. He rubbed his hands together and said suddenly, 'Matter projected from the past? But that would require enormous energy.'

The Doctor nodded. He had an answer to that one

56

too – so simple and so outrageous that it took Tegan's breath away: 'An alien power source.'

In an English country village? Here, at the home of her grandfather? Every instinct Tegan possessed protested against this suggestion – and yet she felt in her heart that it might be correct. The Doctor was usually right about things like that.

'What about Will?' she asked, in a quieter tone.

The Doctor leaned across to peer at the filthy face, torn clothes and battered hands of the peacefully sleeping youth. He smiled. 'A projection, too. And at the moment, a benign one.'

Turlough, in his wanderings, had reached the crack in the wall. He stopped in front of it and pointed at the now gaping split. 'This crack has got larger!' he announced.

The Doctor had already noticed. 'Yes,' he agreed. 'Ominous, isn't it?' He turned to Tegan, who was looking dismal, and slapped her shoulder encouragingly. 'I know,' he said, 'so is the fact that your grandfather has disappeared. I think it's time I sought some answers.'

As a first, peculiar step in that direction, he produced a coin and juggled it behind his back, slipping it with great speed from hand to hand. Watched curiously by Tegan, he then held out his two clenched fists in front of him and, with the most intense concentration, weighed one against the other.

'Where will you look?' Tegan asked.

Making a sudden decision, the Doctor flipped open the fingers of his left hand. It was empty. He gave a disappointed sigh and opened his right hand. There was the coin, nestling in his palm. The decision was made. 'The village,' he said.

'You're always so scientific,' Tegan responded, in a voice edged with sarcasm.

Once his mind was made up the Doctor never wasted

57

time, and now he jumped to his feet and tapped the sleeping Will on the shoulder. 'Come on, Will,' he said briskly, 'you're coming with me.'

'What about us?' Tegan stood up, ready to go with them.

The Doctor shook his head. 'You'll be safer in the TARDIS. And don't argue,' he commanded her, as she opened her mouth to protest. Shouting, 'Will!' over his shoulder, he set off down the nave at a smart pace. Will, still heavy with sleep, stumbled down the aisle and followed him out of the church, blearily rubbing his eyes.

Turlough watched them go, with a resigned smile. He could feel Tegan's frustration, but their instructions had been too precise to misinterpret on purpose.

'You heard the Doctor,' he said, pointing the way to the TARDIS.

Tegan knew there was no alternative but to submit, and with a sigh she turned with Turlough towards the steps to the crypt.

When they had gone, a lump of masonry fell away from the edge of the crack in the wall. It made the gap a little wider still, but nothing could be seen in there – only a dark void which looked as black and deep as outer space.

Almost everything about the churchyard was green. Inside the green fringe of willow trees about the perimeter, the green grass was badly overgrown, tufted and choking the weatherbeaten old gravestones. Many of these were crumbling away, and others were themselves greened over with a growth of moss and lichen. The rest loomed grey-white above the crowding vegetation.

It was peaceful here as the Doctor led Will Chandler towards a row of gravestones. They stood silent as a row of speechless old men, still and warm in the hot sunshine.

Yet around them the air was restlessly throbbing; there was an incessant cawing of rooks and a constant chattering of smaller birds, moving unseen among the flowering grasses and cow parsley and about their hiding places in the willow trees.

Will, too, felt restless. He didn't like this place, and what he saw in it he didn't understand. The implications terrified him. He wanted to run away but the Doctor wouldn't allow it – even now he was pointing at another worn gravestone for Will to look at. The youth crouched obediently down in the grass and pushed a clump of red sorrel aside, so that he could look at the stone properly.

Some lettering was still visible beneath the clinging moss. There were figures – a number . . . Will touched it with his fingers to convince himself that it was real, and the breath sobbed out of him. A date had been carved into the stone: '1850' it said. Yet when Will had shut himself into the priest hole, to escape from the battle that had raged around the church – only hours ago, it seemed – the year was 1643!

'This ain't possible,' he breathed. He was scared to think what it meant if it was true. His eyes misted over.

The Doctor was walking along the other side of the row of gravestones. He watched Will's reactions carefully. 'Look at the others,' he suggested in a gentle, sympathetic voice.

Will stood up. With a last glance at that unbelievable date he moved further down the row, observing the worn, ancient monuments – and every one, thrusting as silently out of the grass as if it was growing there, told a similar story. They were all from the nineteenth century. Will grew more and more agitated; he moved faster and faster until he was running, away from these gravestones and across the path around the church. His feet crunched the gravel. He found another memorial tablet, containing another awesome date, set low down into the wall of the church itself. He crouched down and pretended to examine it.

In reality he was hiding from the Doctor the tears in his eyes. Will wanted to blub like a baby.

Not far away from where he was crouching, the Doctor noticed a small door in the church wall. He tried the handle. The door gave a little. His fingers tightened around the latch, and he pushed harder. With a fall of dust and a creaking noise that echoed hollowly inside, the door opened.

At that moment there was a sound of hooves approaching. A mounted trooper rode around the corner of the church. As soon as the Doctor saw him he pushed the door wide open and hissed, 'Will! Come in here!'

Instantly, as the Doctor disappeared inside, Will left the memorial tablet and ran towards the open door. A second trooper appeared close behind the first; they were walking their horses through the green churchyard. Will's curiosity overcame his fear and he ducked down behind a buttress to watch their approach. This was a foolhardy thing to do, because already the troopers were almost upon him, and now he dared not move again. Just as he thought he must be discovered, the Doctor's hand reached out of the open doorway and yanked him inside.

The Doctor closed the door without making a sound. The horsemen rode on by, quite oblivious of the fact that their quarry was only inches away.

As the Doctor and Will Chandler were going through that side door, not far away from them Tegan and Turlough were entering the TARDIS.

Turlough was in front, and he hurried through the console room without looking around him; but as soon as she was inside the TARDIS Tegan held back, feeling instinctively that something was wrong. There was a noise in the console room, a deep, reverberating tone topped by scattered tinkling sounds which exactly repeated the noises which had afflicted her in the barn.

Bracing herself, she entered the console room – and there, high up on the wall behind the door, she saw lights dancing.

They circled around each other, shimmering and constantly on the move, and the noise which accompanied them grew steadily stronger. Tegan stood rooted to the spot again.

Turlough had heard the noises too. Now he came slowly back into the console room, and stared up at this ghostly manifestation. 'We're too late,' he murmured.

The sound of his voice brought Tegan back to her senses. 'We must tell the Doctor!' she shouted, and ran, putting as much distance as possible between herself and the horrors which lights like these brought with them. Turlough, without Tegan's experience, hesitated. As she had been earlier, he was held spellbound by these flickering, interweaving stars. Then discretion overcame curiosity and he followed Tegan – leaving the lights, and whatever might come out of them, in charge of the TARDIS.

As soon as they were sure that the horsemen were not coming back, the Doctor and Will Chandler began to explore their new surroundings. They had entered the church vestry, a small, bare chamber with stone walls and a flagged floor, which was flooded with light from two arched, latticed windows high up in the walls. Below one of these lay the recumbent stone effigy of a medieval knight.

Will bent over the statue, curious to see whether it was the same effigy which had lain here in 1643. The Doctor, meanwhile, had discovered a large tombstone set among the stone flags of the floor. Intrigued, he ran his fingers over the worn lettering and the outline of a figure which had been scratched into its surface.

'Strange,' he muttered to himself. Then he looked

across at the lost lad he had found in the church. 'Will!' he called softly, 'come and see.'

Will Chandler's head was already buzzing fit to burst with inexplicable wonders. Now, as he shuffled across to the Doctor, his jacket flapping loose, and crouched down beside him, he was prepared for another surprise.

But this one stunned him. His expression changed in quick succession from one of frank, boyish curiosity to awe and then to craven terror. He backed off in a hurry, and whimpered.

'Will?' the Doctor said gently, watching him closely and measuring his reactions. 'What's the matter? Hmmm?' He paused for a moment, and then with great deliberation and care asked him, 'Will . . . what happened in 1643?'

Will had gone down on one knee. He held a hand cupped to his ear as if he was trying to hear something – listening back through centuries to see if the noises he remembered might return. He winced nervously and said, 'Troopers come.'

'No. No.' The Doctor moved close to him. 'Not the troopers, Will. Something else.'

Will backed away further. He was trying to escape the memory. He shuddered. 'Malus come,' he said, in a low and fearful voice. Then his face twitched with terror and he blurted, 'Malus is God o' War, isn't he? Makes fightin' worse! Makes 'em hate more!'

His nerves were in a bad way, but the Doctor had to press him still further to be absolutely sure of what he was saying. 'The Malus is just a superstition, Will,' he suggested.

Will gasped. 'No!' he cried, so emphatically the word came out like a hammer blow. 'I've seen Malus! I've seen it!'

The Doctor watched him keenly, and saw the shadow of the Malus move through his eyes.

* * *

Tegan and Turlough, looking for the Doctor to warn him about the invasion of the TARDIS, ran up the crypt steps and hurried through the church. Outside, they gazed uncertainly around the lines of gravestones in the churchyard.

They had hoped they might find him still exploring the vicinity of the church itself before setting off elsewhere, but the nave had been dark and empty and out here, although it was brighter – brilliant with sunshine, in fact – the churchyard was equally deserted. There was no sign of the Doctor anywhere, and they gazed around in disappointment.

'Now where?' Turlough groaned.

'He said he was going to the village,' Tegan reminded him. Churchyards made her think of ghosts, and more than anything else just now, she wanted to get away from here.

'Right, let's go,' Turlough agreed. 'But watch out for those horsemen.'

Keeping a watchful eye and ear for soldiers and troopers, they headed for the lych-gate and the village, leaving the Doctor and Will behind them, in the vestry.

The Doctor had laid a hand on Will's shoulder, for comfort. It had an instant effect, and soon Will was calmer and quieter, though still tense. His eyes, though, remained distant, brooding on those past events as the Doctor gently prodded him into recalling something which he would much rather forget.

'Will . . .' The Doctor probed as warily as a brain surgeon, for he knew that he was exploring an area of fear so extreme that Will's mind could be snapped by an unwise word. 'Tell me what happened,' he said softly. 'How did it appear?'

Will Chandler allowed the memories to come back. As he did so he stared straight ahead and his eyes dilated. 'There was Roundheads an' Cavaliers,' he murmured.

'An' they wur fightin' in church! And thur was a wind comin' – such a wind!' His breath sobbed and his face twitched violently. 'Then Malus come from nowhere . . .'

He looked at the Doctor with tears in his eyes.

'What did it look like?' The Doctor pointed to the tombstone among the stone flags and placed his finger on the image etched into its surface. 'Did it look like this?'

Will looked at him, pleading to be released from this. The Doctor knew he was falling apart inside, but he had to keep pressing him. 'Did it, Will? Like this?'

With a supremely courageous effort of willpower, the youth nerved himself to look down where the Doctor's finger pointed at a monstrously distorted, grotesque figure, like the carving on the church pulpit. He whimpered. He cried, 'Yes!' and shrank back, turning away his head so that he would not be able to see that terrifying face.

Now the tombstone surprised them both.

As Will turned away the Doctor leaned on it and pressed his fingers into the sculpted face; the stone reacted by moving beneath his hand. He jerked back in astonishment, as the stone swivelled on its axis and rose silently into the air.

Will, looking over his shoulder, drew in his breath sharply: there must be a limit, he thought, to the number of frights he could be expected to take.

'It's all right, Will,' the Doctor soothed him. 'It's all right.' He leaned forward over the hole revealed by the now vertical stone, and saw steps leading down into darkness. 'That's interesting,' he murmured. He produced a torch and peered down into the pit. Then he wagged a finger at the reluctant and terrified youth.

'Come on, Will,' he said.

5

'A Particularly Nasty Game'

The village was deserted. Every street and alley which
Turlough and Tegan warily moved through in their
search for the Doctor was quiet and still. The air was
motionless – even the breeze which had moved the leaves
so gently earlier, seemed to have died away now. The
sun beat down on their heads out of a sky empty of cloud,
and blistered and melted the asphalt surfaces of the
roads under their feet.

At the roadside a telephone kiosk glowed red; the
white-painted walls of the thatched cottages dazzled
their eyes in the strangely luminous atmosphere. It felt
as though the world was burning up – and it seemed that
human life in the village had already vapourised.

Both impressed and disturbed by the stillness, they
came to an uncertain halt. 'It's eerie,' Tegan whispered.
She was very nearly awed into silence herself.

'Where is everyone?' Turlough wanted to hear a voice,
even if it was only his own. He wanted it to activate
something, but the heat soaked it up like blotting paper.

They looked around uneasily, and set off again at a
run, as if by doing so they might startle something in the
village into showing some signs of life. Moving at the
double they came to a T-junction, turned left, and
arrived at a ford, where a river ran across the road in a
sparkling watersplash.

They stopped here to get their breath back. And it was
only then, when they were making no noise themselves,

that they heard the horses behind them. They looked round and saw Joseph Willow and a pair of troopers come cantering out of a side road. As soon as they spotted the two companions, they shouted and spurred their horses into a gallop.

'Oh, no,' Tegan sighed.

'Split up!' Turlough shouted. He ran back up the lane they had just come down, while Tegan bolted forward into the river. She splashed through the ford, and the sudden sensation of cold water dashing against her skin made her shudder.

But their ruse had confused the troopers, who had stopped, uncertain which of them to pursue. After a moment's hesitation, Willow sent his men to chase Turlough, and went after Tegan himself.

As she raced out of the ford Tegan looked back over her shoulder – and stumbled into the arms of Ben Wolsey. The big farmer, who had stepped out of the cover of a narrow alley, caught her as she came running past, and although Tegan struggled and screamed she was helpless in his strong grip. He held her writhing body without effort.

'Let me go!' she shouted, as Willow came riding up.

The Sergeant reined his horse and leaned down towards her. 'Not yet, my dear,' he leered. His pleasure at her predicament made Tegan's skin crawl.

Wolsey sensed it too, and frowned. 'Do you have to enjoy this sort of thing quite so much?' he asked.

Willow tugged angrily at the reins; his horse reared, and clashed its hooves down on the road. 'Just obeying orders, Colonel!' he shouted.

'That's what they all say,' Wolsey commented wryly.

The Sergeant was furious. 'Hah!' he shouted, and savagely spurred his horse back across the ford.

Tegan sensed that the friction between these two was close to breaking out into open hostility; since they were on opposite sides in the war game they would soon have ample excuse to work it out. But for the moment she herself was unable to exploit their quarrel.

There was nothing she could do at all, except accompany Colonel Ben Wolsey in whatever direction he decided to take her.

Ever since Willow had locked her into Wolsey's seventeenth-century parlour, Jane Hampden had been trying to escape. But there was no way out; the windows were securely fastened, Willow had barred the door, and nothing she could do would free either. Wearily she began another round of the room, in case she had missed something.

This time her eyes alighted on an old fighting axe, half-hidden among a display of Civil War weapons on the wall above the fireplace. She cursed herself for failing to realise its potential earlier – with an axe she might be able to smash her way out! She hurried across to the fire, reached up to take the axe – and saw the hunting tapestry move beside her face. It hung near the weapons; now it shifted slightly, as though tugged by a draught of air.

Jane forgot the axe. Excited, she hurried towards a heavy curtain which draped from ceiling to floor at the other side of the tapestry. She tugged at this and discovered that a section of the wooden wall panelling behind it had moved away from the rest. A draught of air was rushing through the gap. Jane pushed the panel; it moved open, like a door. At the other side, a stone passage led away into darkness.

Up to now, Jane had been acting slowly, with the greatest wariness and care. There was no way of telling what she had discovered, or where it might lead. But now she was forced into precipitate action. She heard boots approaching rapidly outside. A voice was raised in anger, then a key turned in the lock. The voice was Sir George Hutchinson's – and Jane panicked.

There was only the one way to escape, and no time for caution, so she pushed the panel wide and ran through the opening into the gloomy passage. She came almost immediately to a spiral staircase; very slowly she began to grope her way down, into almost total darkness.

Behind her, in the room, the key turned in the lock, the bolt was unbarred and the door opened. Followed by two armed troopers, Sir George came in with his mouth open ready to speak to Jane, and for a moment he paused uncertainly, looking around the room with a goldfish expression. Then his eyes alighted on the long curtain blowing back from the wide open panel.

'The fool!' he fumed – a spark of anger which quickly blazed into a full-throated shout of rage at his men. 'After her!' he screamed, adding as they broke into a run, 'We'll need some light! Get a candle!'

The troopers snatched candles from the silver candelabra on the mantelpiece and bent down to light them at the burning logs in the hearth. Then they shielded the guttering flames and followed Sir George into the passage, in pursuit of the schoolteacher.

The Doctor and Will Chandler were also underground, bent almost double to move along the low, narrow passage from the vestry.

In the frail light from the Doctor's torch Will could see only indistinctly its rough, damp sides and roof. They were growing more vague by the minute for the Doctor was moving very fast and Will was lagging further and further behind. It had been like this since their first step from the vestry: the Doctor almost running, swept onward by his eagerness for discovery, while Will, breathless and aching in this constant crouching scuttle, struggled to keep up with him.

Without warning the Doctor stopped suddenly and listened. He beckoned to Will to come nearer, raising a finger for silence. 'Stay close, Will,' he whispered.

Will paused at his side, thankful to have a breather. In the wavering torchlight he could see that the passage broadened just ahead and then opened to a wider area that was like a room hewn out of the rock. At one side of it a spiral staircase led upwards; apart from that the place seemed to be featureless – an empty, eerie cavern in the bowels of the earth.

Then Will heard them: feet scuffing the floor above their heads and then moving slowly and hollowly down the stairs. While he was still translating the sound into words in his mind, the Doctor was diving forward and dragging him into the dark area underneath the stairs. They crouched down there and pressed back against the chill, oozing wall, while the stairs above their heads creaked softly.

Will held his breath and hoped the person would never reach the bottom. But the Doctor was impatient, eager to see who it might be. Suddenly there was another, more distant sound – a voice raised in anger far above them. Then more footsteps scuffed a far-off floor.

Jane Hampden heard the voice while she was still on the stairs. In a panic she looked back towards the passage above, and the last faint spread of light from the parlour, expecting Sir George and his troopers to appear at any second. Not daring to take her eyes off the entrance to the passage, she came down the last stairs backwards.

'Through here!' she heard Sir George shout in a voice brittle with irritation. Another, deeper voice muttered something in reply, then suddenly their footsteps were much closer. Jane shivered. She reached the bottom stair and looked apprehensively around, squinting through the gloom at what seemed to be a room cut out of solid rock.

She almost collapsed with fright when a voice hissed from the darkness beside her: 'Sshh! In here!'

A hand touched her shoulder and she spun round with

a choking cry. Then she saw the Doctor and a youth under the stairs and nearly shouted with relief. The Doctor beckoned and she dived into their hiding place; she was just in time, for Sir George was already coming down the stairs, with the troopers lumbering heavily behind him.

Their candles cast distorted, shifting shadows on the walls and roof. 'Keep that light near!' Sir George snarled. And then, 'We'll catch her before the church.' He stopped at the foot of the staircase and looked back up at the troopers' clumsy descent. 'Move yourselves,' he shouted, 'I don't want this to take all day!'

They hurried across the open area and disappeared into the passage leading to the vestry. Soon the sounds of their footsteps faded away.

Jane let out the breath she had been holding ever since Sir George appeared, and relaxed enough to look curiously at the dirty, queerly-dressed youth who was ducked down beside her. For his part, Will was staring open-mouthed after the running men. He was disturbed and excited by their clothing. 'Them be troopers!' he cried.

The Doctor regretted having to disillusion him. 'No, Will,' he said softly. 'Those are just twentieth-century men, playing a particularly nasty game.'

The small, square box-room high up in Ben Wolsey's farmhouse was bare of furnishings, except for a single chair which stood like a sentinel in the middle of the rough, boarded floor. Light glared in through an uncurtained window.

Willow pushed Tegan into this featureless prison so violently that she staggered clear across the room to the window. He stormed in after her, carrying a green and white, old-fashioned dress over his arm.

'Change into that,' he growled, and threw the dress over the chair.

70

Tegan turned round and faced him squarely. She was fed up with being pushed around, and her face expressed her anger. But it showed fear, too, because there was something extremely nasty about Willow, a viciousness which showed itself especially strongly when he was dealing with people weaker than himself. He had all the hallmarks of an out and out bully.

'Why?' Tegan demanded. She looked at the dress with distaste, hoping to talk him out of it, but Willow was in no mood for a discussion. He marched back to the door. 'Just do as you're told,' he snarled. 'Unless . . .' – he paused in the doorway and leered at her: – 'you want me to do it for you?'

Leaving that possibility hanging like a threat in the still air of the room, he went out and locked the door.

Attempting to escape, Tegan realised, was a non-starter: one glance out of the window at the distance to the ground was enough to convince her that the only way she was going to get out of here was when Willow decided to let her out. He would only do that if she put on this ridiculous garment.

Eventually she picked it up, unwillingly and without enthusiasm. She looked at it and felt a little surge of fear, as she wondered what the point of it could be, and what role she was being commanded to play in this dangerous charade.

Far below Tegan, in the dark passage underneath the farmhouse's foundations, the Doctor, Will and Jane Hampden had just considered it safe to emerge from their hiding place under the staircase when they heard the footsteps coming back and had to dive out of sight again.

The troopers emerged from the tunnel at a trot, shielding the flickering candles with their hands. Sir George was close behind them. He was annoyed and impatient and, as always when he was agitated, he gripped the black spongy ball and worked it ceaselessly with his fingers. He was a man of volatile disposition, always easily aroused, but Jane had never seen him as disturbed as he was now. The agitation which convulsed his mind also racked his body and made his movements seem disjointed, so that he turned this way and that like a puppet.

'She won't get far,' he said as he entered the chamber, 'the village is sealed.' He turned to one of the troopers. 'Get me Sergeant Willow,' he ordered. 'I must see how the preparations are going.' Then he spun round on his heel and snapped at the other man, 'And see that my horse is brought round immediately.'

He was like a man whose nerves were quickly being drawn to their ultimate tension. Without warning he jerked round again and with a wild look in his eyes raced up the stairs and out of sight, with the worried troopers breathing hard at his heels.

In their hiding place under the stairs Jane listened to the departing footsteps and breathed another sigh of relief. Yet she still could not believe they were going to get away with this. Leaning close to the Doctor she whispered, 'It's not like Sir George to give up so easily.'

'Be grateful,' the Doctor replied. He was craning his neck to look up the staircase. 'Where do the steps lead?'

'Colonel Wolsey's house.'

Curiously Jane watched the Doctor leave the safety of their cover to explore the room. He poked about with his torch, examining the walls, the roof, the floor. He had evidently decided they were safe for the time being. He was a strange man, Jane thought, with a remarkable authority; she realised that she trusted his judgment implicitly, and with only a passing hesitation at why she should put her life in the hands of a complete stranger, she followed him out of hiding.

Will had come out too, and was watching the Doctor

scrabbling around on the floor, dreading what he would come up with next.

Jane peered myopically at their surroundings. 'This must be the passage Andrew Verney discovered,' she said, and explained, 'He's our local historian.'

'Yes, Tegan told me.' The Doctor's response was of the vaguest sort, for he had found something on the floor. He crouched on his heels fingering a lump of black, spongy stuff which gave off a metallic sheen in the torchlight. Jane watched him closely, sensing his extreme puzzlement.

Then the Doctor drew in his breath sharply. 'Just a minute,' he exclaimed in a whisper. He stood up and offered the substance to Jane for her to examine. She held it gingerly. Her overwhelming reaction was one of surprise – and uncertainty. The stuff filled her with doubts, for although it was as light as a feather, there was a solidity and weight about it too, and despite its squidginess – she could mould its shape like plasticine – it had a hard, abrasive resilience.

Jane recognised it as the substance Sir George was always fiddling with. This was the first time she had seen it at close quarters, but the closer acquaintance resolved nothing. It only raised questions. The thing was an impossibility – and yet it was here in her hand.

The only thing Jane was sure of was that she had seen nothing like it before. In the absence of clues from the Doctor, all she felt was an overwhelming apprehension – it was like being thrust into a locked, absolutely dark room and wondering what was in there with you. Giving up, she looked at the Doctor and saw from his eager expression that he had some interesting theories which he was dying to expound.

'What is it?' she asked, to please him.

'It's metal.'

Impossible. Jane looked at the substance again and moulded it in her fingers. 'It can't be,' she argued. 'It's all squashy.'

'It's Tinclavic,' the Doctor announced, as if that should settle everything. Jane stared at him, feeling stupid.

'Tinclavic?' she echoed. 'What is that? Where does it come from?'

The Doctor took a deep breath and plunged in at the deep end. 'The planet Raaga,' he said quickly, and watched her mouth fall open. 'Let's go back to the church,' he suggested, and before she could explode he was away, with Will at his heels.

Jane stood rooted to the spot. She stared at the Doctor's retreating back, and gave a frightened glance at the glinting black substance in her hand as if it had just come to life and bitten her.

Feeling strangely alien in the May Queen costume, Tegan stood in front of the latticed window and looked sadly out at the countryside and the yellow-thatched and red-tiled roofs of the village.

Everything was wrong, she thought. Out there some-where was her grandfather, but he might as well have been on another planet. He was missing, and probably in trouble, if not worse. Heaven alone knew where the Doctor and Turlough were, and the TARDIS was probably buried under tons of collapsed stone. On top of that, a youth had crashed out of a wall and another century, everybody was going stark staring mad trying to pretend it *was* that other century and that its horrific war was still going on – and she herself was a prisoner. She had been compelled to wear the clothes of a country girl of the seventeenth century, and so was being forced back in time herself. It was enough to make anybody de-pressed.

Footsteps approached quickly along the corridor out-side. Tegan stiffened with anxiety, and spun round as the door opened. Sergeant Joseph Willow strode in, with a smug expression on his face.

'Don't you ever knock before entering a room?' Tegan asked.

Willow frowned. 'You'd better be careful,' he warned. 'You're beginning to annoy me.'

He came into the middle of the room, clearly surprised by the extent of Tegan's transformation. Instead of her old, gaudy shapeless dress she wore the spring colours of green and white and presented a perfect picture of flourishing, seventeenth-century young womanhood. Her white bonnet dangled gleaming white ribbons beside her cheeks; the fitted dress had a soft green bodice nipped tight at the waist, with puffed shoulders and white flowers; white collar and white skirt completed the picture. Tegan looked as cool and pretty as a wood in springtime – but she did not look happy.

Willow snatched up her old dress from the chair and rolled it into a ball and crushed it in his hands. 'What are you doing?' she cried.

'Those are your clothes now,' Willow smirked, 'compliments of Sir George Hutchinson.' He headed for the door again, then hesitated, turned in the doorway and dropped his bombshell with conspicuous glee. 'You're our Queen of the May,' he smiled.

'What?'

Tegan was dumbfounded. Willow closed the door and locked it behind him. Tegan stood there for a long time, staring at the blank door.

The Doctor stormed up the steps from the passage and ran through the vestry to the church, driven by questions and theories and a host of ideas, some of which were starting to click into place, slotting comfortably into each other like the pieces of a jigsaw, to make the beginnings of a sensible pattern.

However, there were still a lot of pieces missing, and the Doctor could not be certain that the way he was building up the ones that he had was correct. There could be a hundred alternatives; to whittle them down he needed more information, more clues. He headed for the pulpit and its carving, but his attention was attracted by that crack in the wall. It was wider, and the pile of rubble underneath it was larger.

Something was happening inside the wall. The Doctor stared at the crack, puzzled by it, then he hurried over to the stained glass window, and peered up at that, and at the pile of collapsed stone and heavy beams which littered the floor beneath it.

He was still standing there with pursed lips and a puzzled expression when Will and Jane caught him up. 'Slow down!' Jane pleaded. Gasping for breath, she held out the black substance as if it was eating her – and at last asked the question which had been burning in her mind.

'What do you mean, this is from the planet Raaga?'

The Doctor did not answer immediately. Instead, he went back to look again at the pulpit and the cracked wall. He bent to examine the carving, and then told her, in an urgent voice which forbade argument.

'I mean precisely what I say,' he said. 'The Terileptils mine Tinclavic for more or less exclusive use by the people of Hakol . . .' Quite suddenly he softened and turned to Jane with an amused smile, knowing well the effect his words would be having on her. 'That's in the star system Rifter, you know.'

Jane's eyes were wide with disbelief. 'Oh, no,' she cried out in despair, 'I've escaped from one mad man only to find another. Do you expect me to believe what you're saying?'

The Doctor sat down in the front pew and regarded her steadily. 'You take that sample to any metallurgist,' he suggested. 'They'll confirm it isn't of this planet.'

Now it was Jane's turn to study the Doctor in silence. Will, too, was quiet; he rubbed his chin in bafflement and wonder, for this was a conversation stuffed with words he'd never heard of.

Finally, responding to the Doctor's serious and un-shaking gaze, Jane ventured to speak. 'You're serious, aren't you?' she said.

'Never more so.'

She was still confused, however. 'Very well, then,' she conceded, 'for the sake of argument I'll accept what you say. But how did it come to Little Hodcombe?'

The Doctor hesitated. He looked at Jane's cynical expression and wondered how much apparently irrational argument this schoolteacher would be prepared to accept in one session. Then he shrugged. It had to be said, after all.

'On a space vehicle.'

That was the last straw. Cynicism changed gear and accelerated towards hysteria. A broad, pull-the-other-one grin stole across Jane's face and she had to force herself not to laugh out loud. 'A space ship from Hakol landed here? Is that what you're trying to say?'

'More likely a computer controlled reconnaissance probe,' the Doctor said earnestly.

'How silly of me not to know.' Jane's voice was heavy with sarcasm.

Suddenly another piece of the jigsaw slipped into place in the Doctor's mind. He jumped to his feet and asked, 'Tell me, was Andrew Verney engaged in any research concerning the Malus?'

'I believe he was.' Jane's smile faded as she recalled her old friend and his enthusiasm for digging up the past.

The Doctor gave a satisfied sigh. 'That's what must have led him to the tunnel, and the remains of the Hakol probe.'

Will nodded enthusiastically and pressed Jane's arm. 'See? I seed the Malus!' he told her eagerly.

The Doctor laid an arm around Will's shoulder and looked closely into his eyes. 'I believe you Will,' he said. 'My sincerest apologies for ever doubting you.' Will glowed with pride.

Jane desperately wanted to restore some everyday reality to this conversation, and haul it back to a basis she could relate to. If she allowed herself to believe even a quarter of what she had heard, she would soon be as mad as everybody else. 'Doctor,' she pleaded, 'the Malus is a myth, a legend! Some mumbo-jumbo connected with apparitions or something!'

Now that he had got this far, the Doctor had no intention of letting Jane cling to illusions. This was a time for facts, for unvarnished truth.

'That is precisely what Will saw,' he explained firmly. 'On Hakol, psychic energy is a force that has been harnessed in much the same way as electricity is here.'

'But what has that got to do with the Malus legend?'

The Doctor fixed her with an unyielding stare. 'The thing you call the Malus was on board the Hakol probe.'

Now he had her hooked. He saw it happen – he watched the realisation dawn in her eyes. They darkened visibly, and Jane looked uneasily around the church. 'Oh,' she said. 'I see what you mean . . . You mean it's still here!'

Her eyes lit upon the crack in the wall and she hurried across to examine it. 'Doctor,' she whispered, in a voice filled with awe, 'that wasn't here the other day.'

Before the alarmed Doctor could warn her to get away from it, the wall groaned loudly again, and this time there was also a cracking noise which flew around the church like a whiplash, gathering momentum and volume as it went. At the same moment a section of the wall collapsed and caved into the hole. Now it was much wider.

Jane shrieked. She stumbled backwards. Will shuddered and clapped his hands over his ears as a renewed groaning sound squeezed eerily out of the depths of the wall. The Doctor moved forward.

Now wisps of smoke slipped through the crack, oozing out of the wall like bile. Warily the Doctor stretched out his hand towards the wall.

'Don't touch it!' Will yelled. He was very frightened; his shout wailed like a cry of pain, and he was near to tears.

Jane, too, was scared stiff. She felt, rather than heard, faint noises of movements springing from all the dark corners of the church, and there was a smell of gunpowder from the smoke which spilled out of the hole in the wall. The air had turned clammy and cold, raising goosepimples on her skin. 'He's right, Doctor,' she shouted. 'There's suddenly a very strange atmosphere in here!'

Perhaps the Doctor could not hear her because of all the other noises. Perhaps he wasn't listening, because he was so intent upon these strange developments. Whatever the reason, he paid no attention to the cries of Will and Jane.

And suddenly all hell broke loose.

The Doctor was pulling gently at the crack when a huge chunk of plaster came away in his hands. Almost immediately another section blew out of the wall, and now the crack had become a gaping black hole which spouted smoke in billowing, acrid clouds.

'Hello,' the Doctor murmured to himself. He tried to look inside the hole and for a moment thought he could see something which made him catch his breath . . . it was impossible to be sure, but it looked like part of an enormous mouth. High above that there was something green and shining.

A plume of smoke almost choked him. 'Come and have a look at this,' he shouted to the others.

The luminous green light was growing larger. Suddenly it jerked forward towards him. A roaring noise began far down in the wall and sped forward too, moving with the light. The Doctor had to leap out of the way as another chunk of masonry exploded from the wall and whistled past him. Jane screamed.

Something was coming, and coming fast. That deep rumble was roaring towards the surface of the wall at great speed. The green light was coming too – and suddenly it was a colossal eye, glaring at them out of the black socket of the hole.

'No!' Will yelled.

'No!' Jane shouted too. And 'No!' she shrieked again as more plaster was blasted out and another eye loomed in the blackness, high above a huge stone mouth which was twisted wide in the most terrifying leer. It was the same grotesque monster which had been carved on the pulpit and on the vestry tombstone, but many, many times bigger. And it was coming to life before their eyes: moment by moment it grew larger, stretching out and up like an inflating balloon and shooting lumps of plaster and masonry out of the hole with noises like cannonfire.

The Doctor was much too close – right in front of the hole. The noise came screaming to the surface and roared around him like a wind. He clapped his hands over his ears, but it vibrated his eardrums and twisted his face in pain.

'Look out!' Jane yelled – too late, for smoke erupted from the hole, as if the noise had assumed visible form. It poured over the Doctor like a waterfall, and he was obscured instantly.

The noise roared and the smoke billowed, and inside it there were exploding noises as if the wall was disintegrating. The Doctor was inside it too. He had disappeared.

'Doctor . . . !' Jane screamed and screamed.

6

The Awakening

The noise of Jane's screaming echoed around the church until it too was swallowed up by the smoke. At her side, Will Chandler peered towards the wall, which had come so terrifyingly to life with its noise and gushing smoke and those awesome eyes. He whimpered with fear.

Then all at once the smoke began to clear. The rumbling noise subsided to an ominous, steady droning. Through the drifting white cloud, which thinned before their eyes, they saw the Doctor again. He was standing in the exact stance he held when the smoke shrouded him: with his head bent forward slightly, and his hands cupped over his ears, he looked as if he had been turned to stone.

Ignoring the remaining fumes, Jane and Will ran to him. Jane took the Doctor's right arm and tried to lead him away from that obscenity in the wall. He looked stunned. 'Doctor, are you all right?' she cried; he nodded, but she could see that he didn't know where he was or what was happening to him. Now he stumbled and she had to hold him steady. She guided him towards the pews; when his eyes focussed on them he staggered forward and sank down, exhausted.

Will ran around the back of the pew. He crouched down behind the Doctor, bewildered, frightened and near to tears. Jane watched the lad with growing concern, for it seemed to her that Will was not far from snapping altogether. Yet the Doctor was her most immediate problem: he looked shattered. And no wonder! she thought. She removed the green jacket from around her shoulders and put it around his. 'Are you sure you're all right?' she asked him again.

'Yes.' He nodded again, to her great relief.

But a crash made her jump as more plaster flew out of the wall behind her; it seemed to be bursting at the seams. Smoke belched out and the hubbub was renewed, as if the thing inside had got its second wind.

It intrigued Jane as well as repelled her – curiosity bred fascination, and she found herself walking slowly towards the wall. Stones exploded past her and made her jump and shout with fright, but she held her ground. As the Doctor had been, she was nearly hypnotised by what she saw in there: great grey stone nostrils flaring above a grimacing, gigantic mouth, and high above them the green-white brilliance of the eyes. The whole thing looked as if it was made of stone, and yet it couldn't be stone at all; this monstrous thing, which looked most like an enormous magnified medieval gargoyle, was alive.

'It's a face,' she whispered.

It was such an evil face, destructive and filled with hate. As Jane looked at it a feeling of nausea overcame her; her whole being was revolted by the sight and she had to avert her eyes.

'Look at it,' the Doctor insisted. Almost fully recovered, he was leaning forward in the pew and watching her intently. 'Does it look familiar?'

Jane shivered. He wanted her to acknowledge a possibility she had been trying to ignore: that this thing could be the fabled Malus, waking up, struggling to be born in Little Hodcombe of all places, and bringing with it who knew what powers of destruction. Yes, it looked familiar, but she didn't know why, and she could not bear to look at the wall again.

'Yes,' she whispered. 'I . . . I've seen it before.'

82

The Doctor pointed at the pulpit with a gesture that was almost triumphant, for there was always some pleasure to be derived from winning an argument, no matter what the circumstances. 'Look behind you,' he suggested.

Warily, Jane turned around. She had been standing close to the pulpit and her eyes met the carved figure immediately: it seemed to leap up at her and she jerked back with fright. 'But that's a representation of the Devil!' she cried.

'Yes. Isn't it interesting?' The Doctor folded his arms and leaned back in the pew. He smiled, enjoying his little victory, intrigued by the way his theory was developing and the direction in which another piece of the puzzle was dropping into place.

But his triumph was short lived, for another piece of the jigsaw, which he had quite forgotten, unexpectedly jumped out of the place he had made for it. An uneven, scraping noise further down the nave made him spin round, and he saw again the man who had knocked him down in the street – the strange, hooded figure with his devastated face. He stood beside the archway leading to the crypt, watching them and holding Tegan's scarlet handbag clutched to his chest.

'So there you are,' the Doctor breathed.

The man moved suddenly. He came forward, out of the archway, painfully dragging one foot. The Doctor discounted the limp now, for despite being lame this fellow possessed an astonishing turn of speed. The man paused again. He regarded them with his single eye and a stern expression, and as the Doctor looked at him, a light which had been flickering deep inside his eye zoomed suddenly to the surface.

With a shock of horror Jane saw it come right out, breaking out into the air and shattering into fragments, like stars. These too divided into points of light which moved around the man's head and shimmered and twinkled in a constantly changing pattern. 'Who's that?' she breathed, and backed away.

'A psychic projection,' the Doctor explained cryptically. He was on his feet and moving swiftly across to her. 'Over here, Will,' he called. His tone was quietly urgent; Will needed no second telling but ran quickly to the Doctor's side. He stood close beside him, watching the man and the flickering lights, and he was quite ready to run right out of the church, and the village too. It seemed to Will that suddenly there was not a single thing which had not got quite beyond him.

Jane looked intently at the man: how could something so solid be a projection? 'He looks so real,' she whispered.

'To all intents and purposes he is real,' the Doctor replied, but before Jane could argue further the nave was filled with a sound like a wind blowing through from the fields outside. It rose all about them as the man stared in their direction, yet it was not a wind at all. As the light had done, the noise broke into fragments. Splinters of sound stabbed at them from all directions – and they were sounds of battle.

There were trumpets, and fifes and drums. There were guns firing and people shouting; horses squealed with pain. Will started to shake. Beads of sweat stood out on his forehead. Terrified, he looked up at the Doctor for comfort and reassurance. 'I heard that before,' he cried. 'Battle's comin'!'

And before the Doctor could give him the reassurance he so desperately needed, Will cracked. He ran, driven by an all-consuming fear, scuttling to the door at the back of the church as fast as his legs would carry him. The Doctor shouted, 'No, Will! Come back!' but Will took no notice.

He dragged the door open and looked back at them for an instant. 'I's not goin' to war again!' he wailed.

The noise of battle boomed through the church.

Harness jingled, men screamed. The half-blind man glowered with his single staring eye and a pattern of lights shimmered around and through him. It was too much for anybody to stand. 'No!' Will shouted at the top of his voice, and then he was gone.

The lights were now dancing all around the half-blind man. They circled, they writhed like snakes, they built up into a dazzling display. Standing beside the Doctor, Jane was mesmerised by them. Then she caught her breath, unable to believe her eyes, for the figure behind the lights dimmed and then faded away completely. In his place, the image of a soldier appeared and hardened into reality.

He was grey as death. His stance was arrogant and threatening – his right hand rested on his hip and his left gripped the hilt of his sword. His clothes were all grey, as if drained of colour, and his broad hat with its plumed feather was grey too; the skin of his face was pallid and grey-white like parchment.

He stood there, a big, threatening man, watching them from dead eyes.

From the moment he had separated from Tegan, when the horsemen caught up with them, Turlough had been on the run in the village, ducking behind walls and hedges and fences, dodging in and out of gardens, orchards, alleyways, all the time avoiding troopers.

Something was up: they were arriving in ever-increasing numbers, soldiers on foot and troopers on horseback, all going the same way. Turlough was heading in the same direction now, for he was determined to discover what was going on.

He turned the corner of an empty street, ducked down and ran commando-style below the high stone walls of a building which seemed to be the village school. The day had grown hotter than ever. The cloudless sky swelled with the cries of birds, and the air was heavy with the musky scent of the roses festooning garden walls and the thousands of gaudy flowers in the gardens.

Just beyond the school, a sycamore tree overhung a garden wall and shaded the road. Turlough edged towards the tree with the greatest possible stealth, for the road ahead divided to encircle the Village Green; from this he could hear the noise of horses' hooves softly clattering, and a murmur of men's voices. He pressed against the ivy-covered wall and peered around the sycamore to have a look.

The Green was a broad area of grass, which had been burned brown by the sun. There were pools of shade under spreading chestnut trees. It was surrounded by old cottages with warm, colour-washed walls and thatched roofs – and it was bustling with activity. At one side a tall white maypole had been erected; its long ribbons wafted in the breeze. Not far away from it soldiers were bringing armfuls of brushwood and building this into a huge pyre. Mounted troopers patrolled the area.

Turlough frowned: that growing heap of tinder-dry brushwood looked ominous. But while he was still absorbing it all, a hand touched his shoulder. He turned. In the instant of turning he glimpsed the rough, bearded face of a burly trooper, before a fierce blow in the stomach from the man's fist caused him to buckle forward and see only the ground spinning below his eyes. The next moment he had been imprisoned in a searing armlock, and then he was twisted around and frogmarched towards the Green with a vice-like arm pulled so tightly around his throat it was nearly throttling him.

'All right, all right!' he wheezed. 'You've made your point!'

The trooper ignored him. He frogmarched Turlough onto the Green and stopped only when Sir George Hutchinson, who had been overseeing the preparations, cantered across on a big chestnut horse.

Sir George reined his horse to a halt, and from his vantage point glared down at Turlough. He pointed a black-gloved finger at him, and his voice was a paean of triumph. 'One by one,' he shouted, 'you and your companions will return to my fold, and you will never get out again.' He paused, and glanced across the Green, at its feverish activity. 'It's a pity you have seen this,' he said, and then, turning to the trooper, he snarled, 'Lock him up!'

With that Sir George galloped back to his other soldiers. Before Turlough had a chance to protest, he was dragged roughly away.

In the church, the Doctor and Jane felt as if they were being dragged into the vortex of a whirlpool.

The very air around them was being stirred into violence. The monstrous roaring of the Malus in the wall mingled with those shattering sounds of battle to fill the nave with tumult. Smoke and masonry belched from the wall. The flickering lights whirled and dazzled and behind them the image of the Grey Cavalier had solidified into a towering man in plumed hat and long curled wig, with a broad, pointed moustache and a thick beard, who was now moving slowly but threateningly towards them.

Jane's nerve gave way. She was going to run, but the Doctor grabbed her arm. 'Stand perfectly still,' he whispered.

'What is it?' Jane croaked. Her throat had dried up and felt as rough as sandpaper.

'I told you,' the Doctor reminded her. 'It's a psychic projection.'

Jane winced, and submitted. 'It pains me to say it, but I'm sorry I ever doubted you.'

She shivered, and the Doctor returned her jacket and placed it across her shoulders. 'We all learn from our mistakes,' he said drily.

Suddenly, swooping up from nowhere and adding to the already strong impression that the world was being torn apart about their ears, a wind – a real wind this time – rose in the nave. It came up out of silence to roar and howl, and hit the Doctor and Jane like a tidal wave. They staggered under the pressure – Jane would have lost her balance and been dashed to the floor had not the Doctor managed to hold on to her and push her upright again. The power of the wind took their breath away.

'Now what?' Jane gasped.

'More psychic disturbance!' the Doctor shouted above the howling of the wind. And then suddenly there was another thing to worry about: the Cavalier was almost upon them – he loomed up out of the noise and with a rasp of steel drew his sword.

The Doctor retreated, and dragged Jane with him.

'It seems he intends to kill us!' he gasped. 'Make for the underground passage. Run!'

He pushed Jane in the direction of the vestry, and followed close behind her. As they ran up the church, the Malus roared again and lurched inside the wall. It was growing more powerful with every movement. Little by little, it was breaking free.

The trooper frogmarched the almost unconscious Turlough across a deserted courtyard on the edge of the village. His left arm was locked so tightly around Turlough's throat that his air supply was cut to almost nothing, and still he maintained the pressure which forced Turlough's right hand high up between his shoulder blades. Turlough was in desperate straits.

The courtyard was seldom used and the hard earth had grassed over with weeds, over which the trooper now heaved Turlough towards a small, red-brick building at the other side. When they reached it he unbolted the door and threw him inside.

Turlough pitched headlong across the cement floor.

For a moment he lay breathless and dizzy, sprawled full length with his face in the dirt. He heard the door close and the bolt being drawn across, and the trooper's feet march away.

Now, from his exceedingly limited viewpoint, Turlough looked across the floor. He saw a few bales of straw scattered about, and an oil drum. Apart from these the room appeared to be empty. Yet, as he lay regaining his senses, he could hear a soft shuffle of feet on the floor. Then a shadow fell across his face.

Startled, Turlough looked up into the grizzled, unshaven face of an elderly man. He wore twentieth-century clothes – a matter sufficient in itself to mark him as unusual. Turlough pushed himself up on to his elbows and looked at the man fearfully.

'Don't be afraid,' the old man said. He knelt down beside Turlough and laid a hand on his shoulder. Turlough felt easier now that he could see him more clearly: with his baggy old tweed suit, crumpled shirt and tie, untidy hair and mild manner, he looked harmless enough.

Then he said, 'I'm Andrew Verney.' Turlough was looking into the face of Tegan's grandfather.

Jane had run through the church and kept going at top speed through the vestry, down the steps and along the underground passage, but now she was having great trouble keeping pace with the Doctor. He seemed tireless.

She staggered around a bend into yet another gloomy stretch of tunnel. Now she could hardly see the floor, because the Doctor had the torch and he was pulling further ahead with every second.

'Doctor!' she panted. 'Slow down! That thing isn't following us.'

'I need to speak to Sir George,' the Doctor called over his shoulder.

'Haven't you got enough troubles?'

The Doctor stopped and waited for her to catch up. 'Do you know anything about psychic energy?' he asked urgently.

She shook her head. 'You know I don't.'

'Then here's a quick lesson.' He tapped his hand with a finger to emphasise what he was saying. 'It can, of course, occur in many varied forms, but the type of psychic energy here, capable of creating projections, requires a focus point . . .'

Jane was nodding and trying hard to appear as if she understood him, but the Doctor could see she was confused already. 'Oh dear, oh dear,' he tutted. He searched desperately for another word, and found it. 'A *medium*!'

'Ah.' Jane began to catch on at last. 'You mean, as with a poltergeist?'

'Well, yes,' the Doctor agreed, 'but it's a bit more complicated than that. In this case it isn't the medium who is creating the projections, but the Malus. The medium simply gathers all the psychic energy for it to use.' He leaned forward and looked intently into Jane's face, peering at her through the gloom. 'And what, at the moment, is creating the most psychic energy?' he asked.

Jane was puzzled again. She was thinking hard, but along unfamiliar lines, and the Doctor could not wait. 'The war games,' he prompted her.

And light dawned. It exploded like a firework in the darkness of the passage. 'The war games!' Jane almost shouted.

'And who controls the games?'

There was true understanding now. 'Ah,' she nodded. 'You *had* better speak to Sir George.'

The Doctor frowned. 'The trouble is, I don't think he can have any idea what he's doing. The Malus is pure evil. Given enough energy it will not only destroy him, but everything else.' He noticed Jane's glum expression, and brightened up for her sake. 'Cheer up,' he said lightly.

Outside the village, a figure was running across a meadow. He came pounding through waist-high, flowering grasses and weeds with arms flailing and breath heaving, as though the hounds of hell were after him.

It was Will Chandler.

Will hadn't stopped running since he left the church. He still kept glancing behind him in panic and now, as he looked over his shoulder again, his foot slipped into a rabbit hole and he tripped and fell headlong, disappearing from sight among the rank vegetation. Whimpering, he struggled to his feet, stumbled forwards and lurched into a run again.

His chest ached and his face showed the extent of his agony. But the sounds of the battle were still ringing in his ears; he was driven onward by the horrors of the fighting that was still going on inside his head, and nothing could stop him or slow him down.

Will intended to stop when he reached the shelter of the village, and not before.

Tegan stood at another window now, in Ben Wolsey's seventeenth-century parlour. She looked out at his garden, crammed with cottage flowers, whose loveliness expressed all the country pleasures she had hoped to find in her grandfather's home.

She sighed . . . and stealthily moved her hand towards the window catch, which was just above her head. If she could reach that and open the window without the farmer seeing her, she would be out before he could move. Willow had left her in Wolsey's charge while he sought Sir George Hutchinson; since she was not so afraid of this gentle giant as she had been of the sadistic Sergeant, she was more willing to take chances.

But Wolsey, who was standing in front of the fireplace,

had seen Tegan's arm move. He watched it slide almost imperceptibly upwards, and smiled to himself and shook his head. 'You wouldn't get very far if you tried to escape,' he said.

The softly spoken words broke a long silence and startled Tegan. She twisted round and shouted 'What!' at Wolsey, in a voice so harsh it startled her even more than him. There was anger in it, and shattered nerves, and sheer frustration: she was close to breaking down.

Wolsey understood. His tone was sympathetic. 'There are troopers everywhere,' he explained.

'I wouldn't dream of putting you all to so much trouble!' Tegan shouted.

Wolsey seemed embarrassed. His manner was surprisingly uncertain, and even apologetic as he said, 'I rather think we're all Sir George's prisoners at the moment.' Then he smiled reassuringly: 'If it's any comfort to you, your grandfather is safe.'

Relief gushed from Tegan in another shout, this time a cry of pleasure. She ran eagerly to the farmer. 'Then let me see him!' she demanded.

'All in good time.' A coldly calculating voice killed Tegan's happiness in the moment of its birth. She paused in mid-stride as Sir George appeared in the doorway. There was a smirk of victory on his face, and he gestured dramatically with his Cavalier's hat as he came into the room and walked slowly around her, appraising her, examining her in the May Queen dress as if he was looking at the points of a piece of horseflesh. 'You look charming, my dear,' he gloated, 'positively charming.'

The compliment, coming from those eyes and that smile, made Tegan feel unclean. 'Thanks for nothing,' she said, and shrank away from him, angry and embarrassed. 'Can I have my own clothes back, please?'

Sir George leaned towards her. His face was eager and his eyes were as bright as stars. 'But you're to be our

Queen of the May! You must dress the part.' He was purring like a cat now, a sound which made Tegan's skin crawl.

'Look,' she said frantically, 'I'm in no mood for playing silly games!'

'But this isn't a game.'

Suddenly Sir George's tone and expression were deadly serious. They contained an intensity which shook Wolsey into alertness. His next words astonished both of them. 'You,' he said to Tegan, 'are about to take part in an event that will change the future of mankind.'

7

Tegan the Queen

The bare brick walls of the hut had once been painted white; now they were merely dingy. A window protected by iron bars allowed barred sunlight to slant brightly across a floor furnished with forgotten bales of straw.

On one of these Andrew Verney sat. He gazed, without much hope, at Turlough who was testing the window bars for signs of weakness. He had tried them himself, and knew there were none.

'Solid,' Turlough sighed. He moved away from the window, leaned his back against a wall and looked curiously at the old man. 'Why are they keeping you a prisoner here?' he asked.

'Because of what I discovered,' Verney said, returning Turlough's scrutiny with a gaze tinged with sadness. Seeing Turlough's uncomprehending expression, he added, 'Have you been to the church?'

'Oh, yes.' Now Turlough understood only too well. He picked up a dusty oil drum, carried it over to Verney and sat down on it beside him.

Verney shook his head sadly: 'Years of research, to discover that something as evil as the Malus was more than a legend.'

Turlough thought for a moment. 'It wasn't active when you discovered it?'

'No.' Verney gave a wry, helpless smile. 'My mistake was telling Sir George Hutchinson. It was his deranged mind which caused its awakening.'

This sort of talk was making Turlough feel even more nervous and agitated. 'We've got to find a way out of here,' he said urgently. 'We have to let the Doctor know what is happening.'

Verney shrugged. 'But how?' He had tried all the ways there were.

Turlough studied him. The old man had obviously been shaken by his experience and looked tired and worn; if they were going to get out of here it would be up to him to lead the way. He rose from his seat and returned to the barred window. Looking out at the deserted yard, he asked, 'Are there any guards?'

'I don't know.'

'Guard!' Turlough shouted through the window. He hurried to the door. 'Guard!' he shouted again. There was no reply, and no sound of movement outside. It was beginning to look as if they had been abandoned here.

Turlough tested the door. It was pretty solid too, but at least it was wood, and that would splinter if you applied enough pressure. The planks were old and gnarled, with gaps which let in strips of light. He was sure they could be made to give way.

He looked back at Andrew Verney, still sitting wearily on his seat of straw. 'What are you like as a battering ram?' he asked him.

Verney's eyebrows lifted in surprise.

The underground passage connecting the church with the ancient yeoman's farmhouse which now belonged to Ben Wolsey was long, narrow, low, winding and – since it was strewn with rocks, pitted with holes and had to be tackled in a crouching position – arduous.

So it was with a promise of considerable relief for her aching back and trembling legs that Jane Hampden negotiated the very last bend and saw, up ahead, the spiral staircase glimmering faintly in the light of the

Doctor's torch. He smiled over his shoulder to encourage her. 'Not much further!' he called.

'Doctor . . . Wait!' Jane panted. Eager though she was to straighten her back and rest her legs, there were some doubts which she had to clear up before she went a step further. Indeed, her understanding of the situation was still minimal – and if she were honest she would admit that even the bits she thought she knew were pretty hazy. So she was relieved when the Doctor waited for her to catch up, and as soon as she reached him she plunged into the sea of doubts which surrounded her.

'Will said he saw the Malus in 1643 in the church.'

'That's right.'

'Then it's been here for hundreds of years.'

'Long before the Civil War started,' the Doctor agreed. He set off again.

Frustrated, Jane ran after him. She had only just begun. 'Then why has it been dormant for so long?'

The Doctor paused at the foot of the staircase and explained it carefully to her. 'Because it requires a massive force of psychic energy to activate it. When the Civil War came to Little Hodcombe it created precisely that.'

Ah, Jane thought. Another key piece of information brought another lightning flash. She felt the picture filling in, and as they crept quietly up the staircase together she whispered, with more confidence than she had felt at any time, 'And Sir George is trying to recreate the same event?'

'Yes. In every detail. Tegan's grandfather must have told him everything he discovered. It's the only way he knows the Malus will be fully activated.'

The Doctor's attention was beginning to stray, as he wondered what they might find at the top of the stairs, but Jane, tugging urgently at his sleeve, brought him back to the reality of the moment and he looked down at her worried face. 'Doctor,' she said, 'I've just had a terrible thought – the last battle in the war games has to be for real!'

The Doctor grimaced. 'Precisely. The slaughter will be dreadful.'

Jane tugged at his sleeve again. 'You must stop him!'

'Yes, I know,' the Doctor agreed.

But how was that to be done? They reached the top of the stairs. Ahead, a short passage led to a door, through which they could hear a murmur of voices. Prominent among them was the hectoring tone of Sir George Hutchinson. The Doctor put a finger to his lips, waited for Jane to catch him up again, and they approached the door together.

In the parlour, watched by a worried Wolsey, Tegan was arguing heatedly with Sir George across the oak table. She felt she had nothing to lose now, and had thrown caution to the winds.

'History is littered with loons like you,' she shouted, 'but fortunately most of them end up safely locked away!'

Sir George merely laughed, and said in the patronising, half-mocking voice which so infuriated her, 'Insight is often mistaken for madness, my dear.'

Wolsey's agitation suddenly got the better of him, too. He rose to his feet and faced Sir George. 'I didn't realise the power of the Malus was so evil,' he said.

Sir George glared. He pointed a finger at Wolsey's eyes. The finger shook with emotion and his voice was an uncontrolled shout tinged with hysteria. 'Don't worry, Wolsey!' he shouted. 'It will serve us!'

'It will use you,' Tegan countered.

'Tegan is right.'

And so saying, the Doctor pushed aside the heavy curtain drapes and entered the parlour through the secret door, with Jane following close behind him.

For a moment the occupants of the room were struck

97

speechless with surprise. The Doctor marched straight to Tegan's side. His eyes dilated a little at the sight of the dress she was wearing, although his surprise was no greater than Tegan's at seeing him materialise out of a curtain. She knew she should be used to the Doctor's habits by now, but she still found them disconcerting.

The Doctor wasted neither time nor words. He turned at once to Sir George Hutchinson. 'You're energising a force so irresistibly destructive that nothing on Earth can control it,' he told him. 'You must stop the war games.'

Sir George went wild. The signs of obsession and hysteria, and his barely concealed joy at the war games' cruelty had been indications of the road he was taking. Now it seemed that the sudden appearance of the Doctor through the curtain had committed him to that path: something seemed to break loose inside his brain, and those eyes, which before had been unnaturally bright, now burned with an uncontrollable fury.

He aimed his pistol between the Doctor's eyes. 'Stop it? Are you mad?' His voice pitched queerly. 'You speak treason!'

'Fluently,' the Doctor snapped. 'Stop the games!'

Sir George could take no more of this. With a jerky movement he almost threw the pistol at Ben Wolsey. 'Eliminate him, Wolsey,' he screamed. 'Now!' Grabbing his Cavalier hat, and forcing his wayward limbs to obey his wishes, he stormed out of the room.

For a moment after he had gone there was an awkward silence among the remaining occupants. The echoes of Hutchinson's anger hung in the air. Wolsey pointed the pistol uncertainly and without much enthusiasm at the Doctor.

'Put that down, Ben,' Jane said, in the gentlest voice.

Ben Wolsey shook his head, as if trying to clear it of all his illusions about Sir George. 'I don't understand him any more,' he admitted. He looked tired, and his voice was sad; the increasing bewilderment and confusion which he had been feeling for some time had drained him. Now it seemed that everything was beyond him; events had veered out of his control. He was speaking nothing less than the truth: he truly did not understand.

The Doctor felt a lot of sympathy for this kindly, confused man. 'Don't try,' he told him. 'Sir George is under the influence of the Malus.' Then he paused. 'Are you with us, Colonel?'

Weary beyond words, Wolsey sat down heavily. He was no longer pointing the gun at anybody. 'Can you tell me what's going on?' he asked. 'Because I don't know any longer.'

'Doctor!' Tegan interrupted him. She pointed a trembling finger towards a corner of the room, where something only too familiar to her – although new to the others – was happening.

Lights were forming against the wall. This time they developed quickly, much faster than those in the barn, and in no time the first point of brilliance had become a mass of moving stars which danced like fireworks in the corner.

The others gaped, half shocked, half entranced, but shock took over completely when the lights suddenly grouped together in a complex pattern out of which there formed, with a phosphorescent glow, a rapidly stabilising image.

It hung on the wall like an obscenely bloated grey spider. Lights still flickered around it and it was not yet fully formed, but it contained in recognisable form all the features of the Malus – the flaring, sneering nostrils, the sardonic mouth, hair like writhing snakes turned to stone, and the unmistakable aura of evil. While the others stood rooted to the floor, hypnotised by the manifestation, the Doctor moved slowly towards it.

'Be careful.' Tegan shuddered at the memory of her previous encounter; she was not at all pleased that it was happening again.

'That's the thing in the church!' Jane's voice had shrunk to an awed whisper.

'Not quite,' the Doctor decided. He was close to the wall, and was examining the image carefully. 'This is a projection of the parent image. It must be one of several energy gathering points.'

Projection or not, the Doctor was much too close to it for Tegan's comfort. 'Keep away from it,' she pleaded.

The Doctor smiled at her concern. 'It has no force yet.' He spoke reassuringly, but the image seemed to Tegan to pulsate slightly, and to be growing brighter and stronger by the minute.

By now Ben Wolsey was over his initial surprise. Like the practical, rough and ready farmer he was, he now addressed the situation in a practical, down-to-earth way by aiming his pistol at the Malus image as he would at a crow or a rat. It was vermin, and should be treated as such. 'Will this put a stop to it?' he asked.

Holding up his hands to forestall any precipitate action, the Doctor hurried over to him. 'No, it won't,' he said quickly. 'I'm afraid you can't hurt it, because it has no substance.'

The image had the colour and texture of old stone, and to Ben Wolsey it looked as solid as a lump of rock. 'We have to do something,' he said.

The Doctor nodded. 'Yes. We have to prevent the re-enactment. The last battle must be stopped. We must spoil it in any way we can.' He paused, then explained: 'We have to reduce the amount of psychic energy being produced.'

The Doctor's words sent relief flooding through Tegan. 'Then we can forget the May Queen procession!' she cried. But Wolsey shook his head and crushed her rising spirits. 'The cart to take you to the village is already here,' he said.

Disappointed, Tegan looked to the Doctor for support. He was frowning heavily. She knew that look of old – it

100

meant that some fast and furious thinking was going on, so she waited for the plan forming in his mind to surface. Suddenly he gave Wolsey a sharp, appraising glance and asked, 'Will there be guards for the procession?'

Wolsey shook his head. 'No, I'm the only escort. But they will send someone to investigate.'

The Doctor reached his decision. 'Then you make sure that Tegan and Jane get safely back to the church,' he said quickly. 'You can use the underground passage. I must find Turlough and Will. And, er ...' – as he headed for the door he glanced at the image of the Malus growing stronger on the wall – 'Good luck!'

He set out on his search, and left them to their preparations.

Tegan turned to the farmer. 'Do you know where my clothes are?' she asked him.

'I'll fetch them for you,' he promised, 'but stay as you are for the moment.'

'Why?'

He sighed, a picture of the unbounded obsession of Sir George Hutchinson filling his mind. 'Because if you don't turn up in that cart, Hutchinson will turn out the whole village to search for you ... and the Doctor won't stand a chance.'

Tegan's heart sank. She knew he was right, and that she was going to be Little Hodcombe's Queen of the May whether she liked it or not.

Will kept running until he reached the village. Once there, he hid in an orchard to catch his breath and get rid of the painful stitch in his side. Then he crept warily from house to house, from one hiding place to another, gradually making his way towards the Village Green. Every step he took was dangerous, for there were troopers everywhere.

He reached the last cottages surrounding the Green, and looked nervously up and down an open section of road to make sure it was clear. Then he scampered across it like a bolting rabbit and hid on the other side, among the prickly foliage of an overgrown climbing rose which festooned a wooden fence.

After a few moments he had recovered his composure enough to reach up and peer between the pale relics of dead rose blooms towards the Green. The thorny branches criss-crossed his vision like barbed wire. When he saw the Green, his heart nearly stopped.

He caught his breath and bit his lip. Tears rushed to his eyes and his spirits sank to the bottom of his buckled shoes. He could hardly believe his eyes, for what he saw there on the Green *he had seen before*: everything was exactly as it had been when he passed the Village Green on his way to Little Hodcombe church before the terrible battle in 1643.

Everything was happening again – all over again, every detail. There was the tall maypole with its white ribbons whirling gently in the breeze, just as they had then. Near it were the foot-soldiers building up a bonfire for the festivities' fearful climax. And there were the troopers, and the bravely fluttering banner, and the horses and the gaudy uniforms – all the colour and activity which had brightened that day too, before it was crushed, and transformed to screams and blood and ashes.

Will sobbed. On that bright afternoon Squire Hutchinson had cantered about the Green on his big chestnut horse, masterminding the preparation – and here was the new Squire, Sir George – another Hutchinson – dressed in identical Cavalier clothes, riding up to the spot where his Sergeant was telling the soldiers to build the pyre ever higher. 'It's perfect!' Sir George cried triumphantly. Will could hear him clearly, in his hiding place among the roses.

Sir George turned to gaze out across the Green to the houses and streets of the village. He seemed to be looking directly at Will, whose heart thumped madly as he dived down out of sight.

In the narrow, bare hut on the outskirts of the village, Andrew Verney stopped hurling himself at the door and sank exhausted onto a bale of straw. He held his aching shoulder and looked groggily across at Turlough, who gave the door one more battering and then, gasping for breath himself, dropped down beside the old man.

'The door must give way soon,' he groaned.

'Agreed,' Verney said. 'But at the moment all we're doing is wearing out our shoulders.'

Frustrated almost beyond endurance by that stubborn piece of timber, Turlough staggered back on to his feet. 'There's no other way!' he cried, making ready to charge the door again.

As Turlough attempted to break down the door, a farm cart, decorated with flowers and boughs of greenery and pulled by a glistening white horse, was rolling away from Ben Wolsey's farmhouse. Watching farmhands cheered, and women in seventeenth-century clothes threw rose petals over their Queen of the May.

The cart was her royal carriage. Tegan rode high upon it, looking, in that spring-coloured dress, every inch like a queen setting out to greet her subjects. Jane Hampden was on the cart too, as the Queen's companion. The 'carriage' was driven by Ben Wolsey, sitting forward on the box with the reins held loosely in his hands.

Now, as the cart left the farmyard, he flicked the reins and the horse kicked and pulled faster. Villagers lined the route; they waved and threw rose petals. The Queen and her companion exchanged nervous glances and gritted their teeth, steadying themselves for the trials to come.

A fierce heat overlay the village and wrapped itself about the surrounding countryside. The activity which throbbed and stirred inside it made waves which rippled through the fervid air and rolled and crackled like static electricity across the fields, to be drawn as if by a magnet towards the church. Inside it they were swept up into a physical force which charged the Malus with energy.

The energy of a poltergeist may toss objects about a room or cause furniture to travel across a floor. Moment by moment now, the Malus was swelling with the power of a hundred thousand poltergeists. It was making ready to burst free of its bondage in the fabric of Little Hodcombe church.

Still it grew. Energy flushed through it like blood and breath, and packed into muscle and sinew. It drew in more power from the village and still more, and as it swelled smoke poured from its gaping mouth and plaster and masonry spouted out of the wall and flew all over the nave.

After centuries locked in the womb of the church wall, the Malus was being born at last.

The Doctor was worried. His search for Turlough and Will Chandler had taken him through all the streets of the village and he had seen not a sign of either of them. Now he was getting close to the Village Green, the busy sounds of activity up ahead and a monotonous rhythmic clatter of drums told him that very soon he would be able to go no further.

The sun seemed brighter and hotter than ever, and the atmosphere throughout the village was so extraordinarily clear that every detail was sharpened to a bright, luminous precision. The Doctor wished it would reveal his friends, for all his theories about what might have happened to them were unhappy ones.

Suddenly, as he darted across a sunlit road into the cover of an overgrown rose hedge, he saw Will Chandler.

Will squatted on the ground, half hidden by the hedge; he looked as if he had been stunned. He was in shock.

The Doctor crouched down beside him. 'Are you all right?' he asked him gently.

Will nodded, but his expression was lifeless and his eyes seemed to be drawn far back into his head, to be looking inward as if he was seeing something far away in his memory. 'It's just like before,' he muttered. His hand flopped to indicate the scene beyond the hedge.

The Doctor frowned. 'You mean, the last time you saw the Malus?'

Will nodded again, and sighed. 'I's not pleased,' he grunted. He spoke very quietly, as though he were afraid even of the sound of his own voice.

For a moment the Doctor watched him; then he clapped his shoulder sympathetically and rose to look over the hedge and examine the activity on the Green.

This was now so far advanced as to be almost complete. Indeed, there was an impression of readiness, an air of waiting for something to happen. Ready and waiting for what? the Doctor wondered. A crowd of onlookers had gathered there: men, women and children, every one of whom was dressed in seventeenth-century clothes. Not a button or a feather was out of place. There were many more troopers now, and more foot-soldiers. A horse-drawn cart was being led away empty, having deposited its load of brushwood on the pyre.

And now, with a brash military noise two drummers were coming, marching down the lane towards the Green, pounding, pounding their drums with an edgy monotonous rhythm. The people pressed forward with mounting excitement, for the appearance of drummers meant that the Queen of the May would soon be arriving.

All this made a colourful scene; it was like some complicated, carefully-wrought pageant. But the Doctor knew it meant far more than any pageant ever could. It had to be stopped, and quickly, before the Malus took full advantage of the psychic energy being produced and, gorging upon it, grew strong enough to break free of its prison.

Once it had freed itself it would be unstoppable. Something had to be done now. But what? The Doctor crouched back down beside Will, and tried to puzzle it out.

'They burned Queen of the May,' Will mumbled. He winced at the memory. His lips trembled as the event happened all over again in his mind.

Now the Doctor knew the reason for the bonfire: they were going to do it again. A re-enactment, 'correct in every detail,' Sir George had said. He had meant it, too – the war game, as Jane had said, was now being played for real.

'She'd be the toast of Little Hodcombe,' the Doctor joked, trying to reduce the horror and come to terms with it.

Will couldn't do that. The girl's agony had been too great. She writhed inside his head; her skin blistered and blackened, and he could smell it burning. 'It ain't funny,' he said. 'She was screaming.'

'That's nothing to what Tegan would have done,' the Doctor replied grimly. 'Come on, Will.'

Expecting Will to follow, he slipped around the hedge for a closer look at the scene on the Village Green. But Will was too scared to move. He stayed where he was in the hedge, anchored there by his fear, with a burning girl shrieking in his brain.

The Doctor's intention was to duck into the crowd of onlookers, lose himself in the excitement of the May Queen's arrival and then rely on inspiration to fall. But he didn't get even that far. Luck was against him the moment he left the cover of the hedge, for at that moment Sir George Hutchinson jumped on his horse; and as he swung into the saddle he scanned the Green's activities and his glance took in the sight of a man slipping across the road with a wary, half-running and half-walking action and eyes which, like Sir George's own, were trying to see everywhere at once.

Sir George recognised the Doctor immediately and his shout was a great unbalanced cry of both anger and triumph together. 'Stop that man!' he yelled. 'Sergeant Willow, hold him!'

In a trice the Doctor was surrounded by troopers and soldiers; whichever way he turned he saw them running towards him. He attempted to break through the cordon, but he stood no chance; he was overpowered immediately and dragged on to the Green.

8

Stone Monkey

The look of gloating triumph with which Sir George Hutchinson glared down at his enemy was very close to speechless hysteria. He seemed to have lost the use of words, and it was left to his Sergeant to greet their unwilling guest.

Willow emerged from a knot of troopers and approached the Doctor with an arrogant swagger. 'You're just in time for the show,' he sneered. 'You can have a front seat.'

The Doctor, who had decided he didn't care much for the Sergeant, resisted with difficulty the impulse to lash out a foot at him, and for the time being contented himself with an icy stare. Then he looked at the huge pile of brushwood and shuddered; he did not care much for the fate which awaited the May Queen, either.

A roar of excitement swept through the streets leading to the Green. Although he was surrounded by soldiers, the Doctor was held on the crown of the Green, where a very old chestnut tree spread wide its branches; from here he could see between the uniformed bodies of his guard and over the heads of the waiting crowd. He looked across to the road where Will still crouched in the rose hedge, and up a lane lined with waving people.

Down this lane a procession was moving. It was headed by drummers in red coats and steel helmets. They beat the taut drumskins with a never ending rat-ta-tat, rat-ta-ta-ta-ta-tat, over and over and over, and the repeated monotonous rhythm stirred the crowd to ecstasy as the drummers marched down the lane towards them, scuffing their boots in the dust and pounding.

The excitement rippled down the lane like a long, rising wave, and the people shouted and waved and threw flowers at the gaily-coloured cart, which was the coach of their Queen of the May.

Now the Doctor could see past the drummers to the cart itself, and the people closing ranks behind the cart as it passed them. He could see Ben Wolsey driving, leaning forward on the box, looking neither to right nor left but staring straight ahead at the waiting crowd on the Green, and the bonfire, and Sir George standing eagerly in the stirrups on his chestnut horse.

Wolsey's eyes narrowed when he saw the Doctor being held by troopers, but he kept the cart moving steadily forward behind the drummers, to maintain a constant, smooth pace for the May Queen seated behind him.

After the jolting and rolling journey, the Queen of the May no longer sat up so proudly as she had done at the start. In fact, it seemed to the Doctor that now the parade was reaching its climax she had slumped on her throne and was almost slouching. That wasn't like Tegan, who was always spirited, whatever the circumstances.

The Doctor watched the cart arrive and draw to a halt by the side of the Green, and he smiled.

But Sir George Hutchinson, who had been smiling up to now, frowned. He grimaced. Standing up in the stirrups he craned his neck to see over the heads of the encroaching onlookers, and a cloud of anger darkened his face.

A tall trooper, carrying a burning torch, came marching up the Green to station himself at the bonfire, but Sir George took no notice of him, for the villagers' murmurs and shouts of excitment as they ran to surround the cart had suddenly stopped. Now the crowded people hovered uncertainly, and hung back, taken by surprise.

'Something's wrong!' Sir George snarled. Shouting with frustration, he spurred his horse and galloped towards the cart. Sergeant Willow, too, ran forward. The soldiers holding the Doctor dragged him down the Green. The trooper with the burning torch held it high in the air like a salute. Nobody took any notice of him.

Willow reached the cart first. He jumped up on to the boards and strode over to the slouching Queen of the May. Lying limply across the chair which had served as her throne, she looked lifeless. Cursing roundly to himself, Willow snatched away the white, ribboned bonnet: the head so roughly revealed was a ragged, compacted mass of straw. Willow lifted the body and felt the light, limp frame of a dummy. Bewildered, he crushed it in his fingers and dropped it back on the cart. Then he turned in dismay towards Sir George, who was forcing a path through the crowd; he held up the bonnet and pointed to the sad mockery of their May Queen.

Sir George could hardly speak. His face was dark crimson. Veins stood out on his neck. His eyes bulged and the skin on his cheeks twitched as though it was crawling with beetles. Willow stood on the cart and watched him coming to pieces, and could do nothing.

'What's happening?' Sir George finally spluttered.

Ben Wolsey, holding the reins at the ready, turned round on his box and looked Sir George straight in the eye. He too was shocked to see the change in him, but he stood his ground. 'There's your Queen of the May,' he said. 'You can burn her if you wish. This is not as attractive as Tegan, perhaps, but more humane.'

Ben Wolsey, too, had changed. Gone was the diffident, embarrassed, subservient accomplice to the Squire. Now he was an equal, in charge of his own actions and making them count for something; practical and positive because at last he was *doing* something, and taking part in a down-to-earth manoeuvre which he could understand. In such a case Ben Wolsey became a giant of a man, and Sir George, recognising the change, backed away from him. He could scarcely believe what he was hearing; he could not comprehend that all his carefully wrought plans were turning to ashes before his eyes. Then, quite suddenly, it hit him. It hit him hard – his last vestiges of self-control crumbled away, and with them went his reason. Before the eyes of Ben Wolsey and Joseph Willow and all the people around him, Sir George Hutchinson was going mad.

'What are you trying to do?' he screamed at Wolsey. 'Wreck everything?'

Wolsey chose his words deliberately. 'I'm trying to return some sanity to these proceedings,' he said.

The implications were lost on Sir George. He seemed to be past understanding anything. Holding his head as if it were about to burst, he cried out, 'You've ruined it! You've ruined everything!' With an agonised expression he turned to his Sergeant. 'Kill him!' he shouted. Then he wheeled his horse away.

Wolsey had been expecting this and was ready for it. Although surrounded by enemies he felt ice-cool; he was seeing things very clearly and he knew that Willow would now go for his sword. He was right, but Willow only got as far as laying his hand on the hilt when Wolsey yelled and whipped up the horse and the cart lurched forward.

Willow lost his balance completely and fell sprawling from the cart. He lay winded on the ground.

While this was going on the Doctor had tried to take advantage of the confusion to slip away from his captors. Unfortunately for him, the soldiers had grown even more terrified of their leader in his manic condition than they had been before, and they were making doubly sure that his fury was not increased by the loss of his prisoner. So instead of their grip on the Doctor slackening it increased, and his chances of escape were less than ever.

Then he saw Will Chandler.

Will had watched the events on the Green with an overwhelming joy when he saw that by some miracle the sacrificial burning of the May Queen had been avoided. He had breathed a big sigh of relief and edged forward to see if he could help his friends; now he saw the Doctor's predicament at the moment the Doctor saw him.

'Over here, Will!' the Doctor shouted.

Will ran.

What happened then occurred so quickly that afterwards Will was unable to separate one event from another. When he started to run towards the Doctor he had not the vaguest notion of how he was going to help him. But as he crossed over to the Green he saw, out of the corner of his eye, the trooper carrying the burning torch. Almost without thinking, he changed direction and dived at him.

Although the trooper was twice Will's size the charge took him completely by surprise, and he staggered backwards and dropped the torch. It rolled across the grass.

Will picked it up. The heat scorched his fingers, but he gritted his teeth and holding the torch firmly with both hands, began to whirl it around his head. The swinging flames made a peculiar roaring noise, like water tumbling over a weir. Will was a fearsome sight as he advanced on the soldiers holding the Doctor, with sweat running down his forehead, a look of stubborn determination on his face, and the torch flying and roaring in his hands. The soldiers scattered in fright as it flared towards them – and the Doctor was free.

But now Sir George Hutchinson was galloping across, yelling with fury. Without thinking Will turned to face him, too. He was still whirling the burning torch about his head. With sparks flying in all directions, the flames swept round towards Sir George's horse. It panicked and pulled its head away from the heat, rearing high in the air and throwing Sir George out of the saddle. He fell head first to the ground, and lay very still.

Will hoped he had broken his neck. But there was no time to find out, because troopers and soldiers were running towards them on every side.

Ben Wolsey, whipping the cart to a great speed, reached them first. The Doctor jumped up beside him and shouted to Will, who hurled the torch at the approaching soldiers and pulled himself up into the cart too. And they were off.

'Back to the church!' the Doctor shouted to Wolsey. Then, with a sincere 'Thank you' to the farmer and the youth, he picked up the straw May Queen and tossed it at their pursuers.

The Green was in turmoil. There was much shouting and swearing and everywhere people were running aimlessly about. Holding on tightly to the sides of the wildly swinging cart, Will watched them receding into the distance. He was disappointed to see both Sir George and Sergeant Willow climbing groggily to their feet, and he heard the screaming hysteria in Sir George Hutchinson's voice as he shook his fist at the cart and yelled, 'After them! After them!'

Willow began to run.

Inside the church, the Malus fell silent the moment Sir George toppled from his horse. Up to that moment it had surged and pulsated with the energy produced by the excitement of the procession, lurching and pushing itself ever more free of its restraints; evidence of its success lay all around in the piles of shattered masonry, and in the wisps of smoke which still hung about the roof of the nave.

But now the Malus was still. It brooded in silence, working out its next move . . .

Across the village, the door of the hut in the quiet, isolated courtyard was splintering. It bulged outwards. It heaved against the drawn bolt as it was hammered and battered from inside.

All at once a panel gave way under the constant pounding. Then another split open, and another, until with a ragged cracking noise the whole door broke away from its hinges, the bolt flew off and Turlough and Andrew Verney tumbled out into the bright sunshine.

Carried forward by the impetus of the final charge, they staggered across the yard, and then stood swaying and

113

blinking in the dazzling light, nursing their bruised shoulders. Verney clutched his baggy tweed hat. 'We must get to the church,' he said. 'We have to destroy the Malus before it becomes too powerful.'

Turlough frowned. As an idea, that seemed to him to be a little on the bold side, not to say foolhardy. 'Let's find the Doctor first,' he suggested.

The old man was adamant. 'We haven't got the time,' he insisted. 'We could spend the whole day looking for him. Come on . . .'

To prevent further argument he set off running, at an old man's stately trot – leaving Turlough no option but to follow him.

Wolsey drove the cart like a man possessed. The Doctor and Will had to hold on grimly to prevent themselves being thrown out as the horse kicked its heels and the cart jerked and shook, jolted and rattled along a rutted track through the fields which, the farmer swore, was a short cut to the church. Now and then they could hear shouting behind them; in the distance soldiers were running, and horsemen galloped along the skyline.

They arrived at the lych-gate just in time. Wolsey reined in his valiant horse, stopped the cart and they jumped down. Will staggered and had some difficulty keeping his balance, and he felt that something inside him had shaken loose, but there was no time for self-examination and he had to run his fastest to keep up with the Doctor and Ben Wolsey. They were heading around the side of the church and making for the vestry; Will dreaded going back inside.

The Doctor pushed open the vestry door with a crash and burst in, giving a big fright to Tegan and Jane, who had just emerged from the underground passage. Jane was closing the tombstone entrance to the tunnel. Tegan, happy to be wearing her old dress again, was warily opening the door to the nave.

The Doctor was delighted to see them. He nodded with

114

satisfaction but had no time to spare for congratulations. 'Come along, we've a lot to do,' he said, hustling them as he rushed through to the nave, followed by Ben Wolsey and Will Chandler.

Jane watched them go, and shrugged. Given time, she thought, she could get used to most things, but she doubted if she could ever get used to the Doctor.

The nave hummed and vibrated with a low, buzzing sound. It was like the noise of a furnace – the sound flames make as they rush up a chimney when it is on fire.

The Malus's brooding silence had ended; the fury now erupting through the village had urged it into life again and it was steadily ingesting the power it needed to make its final bid for freedom. Those great nostrils flared with a wild anger; the eyes glinted and flashed; the mouth gaped – a vast, shark-like maw that looked as if it would swallow the world.

As he ran through the church the Doctor glanced at the disappearing wall, and saw that time was running out on them. 'Hurry!' he shouted.

They kept close together, running one after the other up the nave and through the archway, then down the steps to the rubble-strewn crypt.

The Malus watched them go by. Soon – very soon now – the time would come when no one would ever be able to pass it again. Soon no life would be able to survive in its vicinity. The green, phosphorescent eyes pulsed with the light of its coming triumph.

The Doctor ran down the steps to the crypt three at a time. At the bottom he paused to take the torch from his pocket; he switched it on and set off towards the TARDIS, only to stop again suddenly. He turned to Tegan. 'You didn't close the door,' he snapped.

'There was no point,' she protested. 'Something was already inside.' What was the point in trying to explain now

115

that they had been looking for the Doctor to tell him about this when she had been abducted and Turlough had disappeared? He was too angry to listen.

'This is all we need,' he scowled. He paused for a moment, then made up his mind and marched inside. Tegan and Will hurried in close behind him.

Will had given up being surprised. When he had been bobbing and swinging about in the cart and feeling sure that his bones were splintering inside him, he had made up his mind that if he survived he would take everything in his stride from now on. He had discovered that when absolutely everything is extraordinary, nothing is astonishing any more. Running into a blue box, therefore, was simply another wonder to be accepted without demur, and he shrugged as he ran in through its door, as though this sort of thing happened to him every day.

It was not so with Jane Hampden and Ben Wolsey, however. They looked at the TARDIS in wonder, approached it warily, gazed at each other with a wild surmise – then they, too, shrugged and went inside it.

Once inside they – and Will Chandler, despite his newly-made resolution – were more overwhelmed than ever. For a moment they were struck dumb by the sheer size and technology of the TARDIS's interior. But, as Tegan had found out so many times before, there was no time for discussing trivial matters like the feeling that they had just walked into Aladdin's cave, for Aladdin himself was already fully occupied at a large illuminated console, pounding switches as fast as his fingers would move.

The Doctor was looking for instantaneous results and, when they didn't come, he threw up his hands in disgust. He pressed more buttons – and a low, steady hum of machinery was heard. Then, without turning round he pointed backwards and upwards to the wall above the door. 'Quietly now,' he whispered. 'Don't alarm it.'

Startled, they looked up and saw the lights which had alarmed Tegan and Turlough earlier. They were still shimmering, still moving in a seemingly random pattern, but there was something else now: inside the lights, clinging to the wall, was the obese, bloated, spider-like shape of another rapidly-forming Malus clone.

It was like the one which had invaded Wolsey's house, except that if possible it was even uglier. Its head, much too large for its body, possessed hair like clustering snakes, bulging eyes, a misshapen chin and vicious, shark-like teeth. Its arms and legs were thin and over-long, and the fingers and toes were attenuated and spindly like the bones of a deformed skeleton. There was a ribbed, scaly tail which helped it to cling to the wall like a stone monkey.

And it was coming to life.

They were too amazed to speak. The heavy atmosphere of the console room seemed doom-laden and full of threat – an impression which was strengthened by the urgency with which the Doctor was flying from one bank of instruments to another.

It was Tegan who dared to speak first. 'What are you doing?' she asked him.

Stopping his frantic activity for a moment, the Doctor surveyed his handiwork, and frowned. 'If I can lock the signal conversion unit on to the frequency of the psychic energy feeding it, I might be able to direct the Malus.'

Wolsey looked at him sharply. 'Is that possible?'

'Well, there's a remote chance.' The Doctor did not sound very optimistic. As an afterthought, he operated the scanner screen mechanism; the shield lifted silently and showed Joseph Willow and a trooper creeping across the crypt towards them.

'Doctor!' Tegan shouted.

The Doctor had already seen them. 'Ah,' he said quietly, 'perhaps you should close the door.'

Wolsey gazed at the screen. 'They didn't waste much time,' he said, frowning. He was very disappointed that his adversary had caught up with them so quickly.

Jane, intrigued, watched Tegan run to the console to

operate the door lever. The door slid shut. Tegan breathed a sigh of relief: they were safe for the moment. Except, of course, for that thing on the wall . . . She looked at it and shuddered. It was growing more lively by the second.

Joseph Willow and the trooper moved quietly through the rubble of the crypt towards a strange blue shape which loomed out of the shadows ahead of them. They picked their way slowly and warily, taking great care to make no sound.

When they reached it they stood and gaped in disbelief. 'A police box?' Willow grunted. How could they all have crowded into a police box? He looked around uneasily, to make sure his quarry was not hiding somewhere else in the crypt. Then he drew his sword; holding it in readiness, he nodded to the trooper to open the door.

Obediently the man approached the TARDIS and tried unsuccessfully to make the door move so much as a fraction of an inch. He rattled the handle helplessly, then turned to his Sergeant. 'It's locked,' he said.

This was the last straw for Willow, the final frustration which snapped his patience. With a head near to bursting because of the humiliations and disappointments of the afternoon, he screamed furiously at the trooper: 'Well, don't just stand there! Break it open!'

The man looked uncertainly at him, then removed his helmet, tossed it down among the fallen masonry and searched for a door-breaking implement. Soon he found a heavy piece of timber to use as a battering ram. He staggered with it to the TARDIS, held it in front of him and charged against the door.

9

Servant of the Malus

Inside the TARDIS, that noise became a dull, monotonous, ceaseless thudding. The reverberations were ominous and hypnotic, and with the exception of the Doctor all the occupants stared at the scanner screen, watching with bated breath the progress of their enemies outside.

The Doctor was puzzling over monitors and switches and levers. He moved from one set of controls and dials to another, making adjustments and corrections, setting up sequences in a complicated and ingenious program which only he could understand.

All at once there came a weird elephantine trumpeting noise. It vibrated through the console room, and seemed to Tegan to be like the roaring of the Malus heard through a long tunnel. Instinctively she glanced away from the scanner screen and up at the image clinging to the wall beside the door, and gasped at what she saw.

'Doctor!' she cried, 'the Malus!'

They all looked and shuddered. The image had not only grown suddenly; it was lifting itself off the wall now, as if making itself ready to leap at them. Its head jerked sideways and half turned towards them. Energy surged through the flickering lights, which crackled and pumped strength into its ugly body. Soon it would be strong enough to support independent movement, the Doctor saw – and then what? The prospect was unwholesome, and frightening.

The Doctor took in the situation at a glance. His

movements at the console, already hurried, became feverish. He pulled a lever, hammered a switch with his fist – and waited, tapping his fingers with frustration at the delayed reaction. He was hopping about on his toes like a runner dying to launch himself into a race. Every split second counted now.

Wolsey, who had been watching him closely, felt the Doctor's increasing anxiety. 'Won't it work?' he asked.

The Doctor fairly shouted at him. 'It takes time!' he cried. 'Excuse me, Colonel.' He pushed the farmer aside in his eagerness to reach another set of switches at the far end of the console. He'd forgotten those; no wonder there was a delay. He glared at Jane; she was in his way, although she moved out of it quickly when she saw that impatient look on his face.

The trumpeting increased in volume and rose in pitch. It transferred their attention away from the Doctor, leaving him free to get on with his complex programming, to the hypnotically ugly growth above their heads. It was moving constantly now, shaking its head, lifting itself from the wall. It was nursing its energy for the moment when, with its parent in the church, it would truly be born again, and they could be released to take over the TARDIS and the village, and cause the wholesale destruction which had been the sole purpose behind their creation.

And meanwhile, the ceaseless hammering on the door continued unabated, as the Doctor's pursuers tried to batter their way in.

Inside the church, the Malus was also building itself up for the final, all-conquering effort that would ensure its release. The nave shook with its increasingly powerful vibrations, and echoed with the noise as it roared and spat smoke from the deep, dark cavern of its mouth.

It was into this hellish din that Turlough and Andrew Verney ran unawares, when they opened the door of the church and came hurrying through the pews.

'Oh, no!' Verney groaned. The sight of the gigantic Malus taking over the church and springing to life in his beloved village overwhelmed him. He held an arm over his eyes and staggered away from it; he would have fallen if Turlough had not steadied him.

'Let's find the Doctor,' Turlough suggested. 'There's nothing we can do.'

He guided the trembling, shocked old man back towards the main door. Then he stopped, and listened carefully. Through the roaring of the Malus they heard another, deeper noise, repeated over and over; it echoed up to them from the crypt.

'What's that?' Verney whispered.

Turlough looked at him. He was listening hard, trying to extract meaning from the sound. His face was drawn and worried-looking, and the old man felt his body go rigid with anxiety. 'The TARDIS is in the crypt,' Turlough said quietly. 'I think we should take a look.'

Inside the TARDIS, the Doctor, working frantically at the console, was in the closing stages of establishing a program which might – success was by no means certain – give them some defence against the growing power of the Malus. But he was losing the race, as the gasps and moans of his companions warned him.

The image, like the mythical spider which invented its own existence, was spinning itself out of those tinkling, whirling lights. And it had almost accomplished its task: it moved its head freely now, craning further and further round to glare at the Doctor, as if it sensed that he was the real enemy, the one person it needed to fear.

The trumpeting sounds hardened and the lights spun with greater gusto. Tegan, who had more experience of these manifestations than any of the others, detected a

121

note of triumph creeping in; and then suddenly the head jerked, broke free of all restraint and swung round to face the console.

'Doctor!' she shouted in warning.

The image watched the Doctor closely now; it seemed tense and drawn back, ready to spring. It looked to Tegan for all the world like some hideously deformed grey bat up there on the wall, waiting for the right moment to launch itself into flight.

The Doctor glanced upwards. 'I know,' he breathed quietly. He was very tense too, aware always that the image was only part of their problems. The heavy battering outside was still continuing, and it was just a matter of time before the door collapsed and let their enemies in.

The Malus image shifted threateningly. The Doctor held up his hands for them to be patient and stop distracting him. 'It senses what I'm about!' he cried anxiously. 'Now everybody stay perfectly calm and still!'

Concentrating furiously in the silence which followed, he was able to make his final set of calculations. Now he approached the last bank of controls.

In the church the Malus closed its eyes and fell silent again. The nave became ominously still, as if it too was breathlessly waiting. Smoke hung suspended about the pillars and floated in wisps and silent streams across the vaulted roof; somewhere a small piece of plaster, shaken out of its anchorage by the last bout of noise, finally edged loose and clattered to the floor. The sound crashed through the silence like a pistol shot.

The dull thudding noise still vibrated up from the crypt, but here now all sounds were held in suspension, taken up into the silent brooding of the alien monster, which had grown so large it seemed to occupy the whole church wall. The Malus was listening. Sensing the mischief being worked against it by its enemy in the crypt, it had probed out psychic antennae to link into his thoughts.

All at once it realised what the Doctor was planning, and the full extent of the threat to its ambitions became clear. In that instant its eyes flipped open and glinted with anger; it roared and swung forward in the wall, shaking itself free before the Doctor's program could be completed. There was panic in the jerky movements, and desperation in the deafening roar and engulfing smoke which poured out of it.

That roar shook the church to its foundations. It rumbled through the crypt and reverberated inside the fabric of the TARDIS. It summoned up the spirits of the churchyard dead, and rolled across the fields surrounding the church, creating a tidal airwave which rushed through the village to the Green and its faithful servant, Sir George Hutchinson.

The Green had become quiet. The troopers and soldiers had all gone to scour the village for the strangers. Most of the villagers had departed in dismay, appalled by the turn of events and the disintegration of Sir George Hutchinson.

When he had regained consciousness, Sir George had staggered around the Green, shouting, screaming, threatening everybody. He waved his sword about and almost decapitated an unwary villager, who had been looking forward to an enjoyable afternoon's entertainment beside the bonfire. That was more than enough for most of the onlookers. The party was over before it had begun, so they went home and left the Green to Sir George and his madness.

Only a few bystanders remained, talking quietly among themselves and keeping a wary eye on Sir George in case he should erupt again. But he had been quiet for some time now. He wandered about dazed and uncertain, as if he didn't know where he was.

Now he noticed his horse, peacefully grazing under the chestnut tree, and approached it with a tired, un-balanced stagger. He picked up the reins and dragged himself wearily into the saddle. He was sitting there, limp and looking only half-conscious, when the cry of the Malus reached him.

He heard it coming, like a tidal wave moving in from the horizon at an incredible speed. It came roaring through the sunlit afternoon, a vast towering ridge of sound which blotted out sky and sun and then every-thing in the world.

Suddenly it was upon him. It engulfed his mind. Now he felt he was inside the noise, it had swallowed him up and there was nothing anywhere but this roaring, louder than it was possible for a mind to hold.

The impact stunned him. He stared wildly into the air. Then his eyes started from his head and his mouth creased in pain; his hands went to his ears and held his head against the buffeting, and he screamed. He cried out the one word, 'No . . . !' in a long, drawn-out shriek of pain and terror as the Malus sucked the mind out of him.

Sir George was its true servant now. He was com-pletely in its power – far more than he had ever thought a man could be controlled by an outside force. The Malus commanded, and Sir George Hutchinson obeyed; no longer had he any choice in the matter.

The people on the Green, startled by his wailing cry, were watching him even more warily now. 'Out of the way!' he yelled at them. 'I must get to the church!'

But before they could move, he dug his heels into the horse's flanks and galloped through the shade of the chestnut tree into the hard sunlight on the Green, scattering them in all directions.

Sir George Hutchinson, the once proud owner of Little Hodcombe, was answering the call of his new master.

* * *

Turlough and Andrew Verney sidled down the steps to the crypt. They pressed their backs into the shadow of the wall and kept strict silence, all the time watching the two figures across the crypt trying to break into the TARDIS.

The Malus's roar had disturbed them too, but there was no time to worry about it because the trooper hammering away at the door of the TARDIS was going to have it down soon. Willow, who had sensed that success was very near, stood by with his sword held in readiness, prepared to charge the moment it gave way.

When they reached the foot of the steps Turlough led Verney around the edge of the crypt, in the shadows, again crouching close to the wall. Once he stopped to allow the old man to catch up with him. 'What do we do?' Verney whispered in his ear.

'Sssh!' Turlough pressed a finger to his lips, then groped around the floor and picked up a stone hefty enough to fell a man with a single blow. He weighed it in his hand and gave Verney a meaningful look. The elderly man nodded anxiously and found a stone to arm himself.

As soon as they were ready, they glanced at each other for confirmation and launched themselves across the remaining yards of rubble-strewn floor at Willow and the trooper. By the time they were heard coming it was too late.

As their enemies turned round with surprised faces, Turlough fell upon Joseph Willow. He brought down the raised stone with all his strength and gave the Sergeant a crushing blow across the side of his head. A split-second later Verney, with the greatest gusto, performed the same operation on the trooper. Willow and the trooper grunted under the impact of the stones. They were unconscious before they hit the ground.

Panting for breath, Turlough and Andrew Verney looked at each other and smiled a little smile of victory.

* * *

Inside the TARDIS the struggle had reached its moment of resolution. Victory was about to be won – or lost – for the Malus image was preparing to leap at the Doctor, and the Doctor had completed his program.

Now, with a lot of deliberation and even more hope, he pressed a final set of switches. Instantly a low, clicking, electronic hum filled the console room. There was a sensation of air vibrating very deeply. 'That's it!' the Doctor cried, with a smile of satisfaction and relief.

Tegan gave him a pleading look. 'Can you control the Malus?'

'Ah, not quite,' the Doctor admitted. 'But it can no longer fuel itself from the turmoil in the village.'

Now he permitted himself a glance at the Malus clone, which was glaring down at him from the wall. He had cut off its power source too, and the sudden deprivation of its life blood could have dramatic consequences – eventually, he thought, the image might collapse in upon itself like a deflating balloon.

However, the results came sooner, and even more dramatically, than he had expected. Almost immediately the image slumped and there came a blood-curdling, retching noise from inside it. Lumps of vivid green mucus blew out of its mouth and dribbled from its eyes.

It was a sight so obscene that despite their unbounded relief that the Doctor's efforts had worked this far, the onlookers winced with disgust. The green mucus poured and spouted, and the image began to implode. Tegan, feeling very sick, turned away her head.

Jane, who had also averted her head, was staring at the scanner screen, her eyes wide with wonder. Only moments ago the screen had shown Willow and the trooper battering their way into the TARDIS: now, large as life, there stood in their place the gasping and bemused figures of Turlough and Andrew Verney.

'Doctor – look!'

The Doctor followed her pointing finger. His eyes

absorbed at a glance the prone figures of their enemies and the weary but triumphant stance of their friends, and he grinned with pleasure. He gave a last glance at the now rapidly-shrinking image, retching in its death agony. 'I think it's time we left this thing to die in peace,' he said, and led them all out of the TARDIS.

As the Doctor came out through the door he smiled at the sight of the old man bending over the two unconscious bodies, and Turlough standing guard over him. 'Turlough! Well done!' he cried.

Tegan pushed past him. Scarcely able to believe her good fortune, she paused for a moment to look at the man she had begun to think she might never see again. 'Grandfather!' she shouted, and almost crying with happiness, she ran towards the crouching figure. Verney looked up at the sound of her voice, pulled himself to his feet and held out his arms.

'Tegan, my dear!' he said happily, and kissed her warmly on the cheek.

The Doctor, already racing towards the steps to the church while the others were still tumbling out of the TARDIS, cut short their reunion embrace. 'Save your greetings until later,' he called.

Ben Wolsey ran past them. Tegan looked at her grandfather. 'Never a dull moment,' she shrugged. They smiled at each other, and ran after the Doctor and Wolsey. Jane Hampden was close behind them. Will Chandler, sticking to his resolution of not trying to understand anything at all and letting himself be carried along from one crisis to another, ran at her heels. Turlough, with a last glance of satisfaction at his fallen foes, brought up the rear.

Although they hurried to follow the Doctor, they were all afraid of what they were going to have to face in the church. As they walked warily into the small chapel at the top of the steps, the roaring of the Malus, the clouds of smoke and the acrid stench of destruction hit them;

they had to force themselves to go further, and steel their nerves to turn through the archway and into the nave.

The wall beyond the pulpit was now all Malus. The gigantic head turned its eyes and loured at them as they came in. It trembled and shook with rage and lurched forward, still trying desperately to break free. Every effort, though, used up energy, and the Doctor had cut off its power source in the village. With eyes narrowed to slits it watched their every move.

Wolsey, who was keeping close to the Doctor's shoulder, blanched at the sight. 'Now what?' he asked. The Doctor, searching for inspiration, was looking at the Malus as intently as it was at him. 'I don't know, yet,' he admitted.

'Doctor . . .' Turlough pointed towards the top of the nave. The Doctor turned away from the Malus to look, and stiffened with surprise.

Three troopers had appeared, and were moving slowly down the nave towards them. They were no ordinary soldiers, though – and they were certainly not twentieth-century villagers in disguise. Everything about them was drained of colour. The helmets, breastplates and tunics of Parliamentarian soldiers, which they all were, showed an identical shade of lifeless, greyish white; their stern, bloodless faces were the faces of men roused from their graves in the service of the Malus.

Verney shuddered. 'Where did they come from?'

'The Malus,' the Doctor whispered. He watched the ghostly troopers' relentless progress: they marched down the nave in eerie, silent unison. He felt the tension of his companions, their growing suspense as they started to move backwards.

Now the troopers' slow, marching motion was propelled and echoed by the hollow beating of a drum.

Jane looked doubtfully at the Doctor. 'They're psychic projections?' He nodded.

'I'd feel happier with a gun,' Wolsey announced. He

128

was a true man of the soil, forthright and practical, to whom the possession of the right tool for the job always gave a sense of comfort and well-being. But there was no tool for this job. 'It wouldn't make any difference,' Tegan told him. 'They're not real.'

'They look solid enough to me,' Wolsey muttered.

'This is the Malus's last line of defence,' the Doctor explained. 'And they'll kill just as effectively as any living thing.'

The unseen drum throbbed, and the troopers marched on in absolute unison. Their austere and forbidding faces stared at the Doctor and his companions. There was no hatred in them, but nor was there any compassion; they were dead faces, with no expression at all. The little, frightened group retreated before them, moving closer and closer to the broken altar.

In the crypt below them, another trooper was stirring. The man Andrew Verney had felled with his stone had begun to groan and murmur to himself. Now, with much grunting and puffing, he pushed himself up to his knees.

He was still only half conscious. He knelt for a while, swaying groggily and holding his aching shoulder; gradually his head cleared a little – enough for him to notice Willow's body lying on the floor beside him. He bent over it and pulled it up to look at the Sergeant's face. Willow was still out cold.

The trooper let him slump again as dizziness and nausea came flooding back. He shook his head and mumbled to himself. He couldn't remember where he was, or what he was supposed to be doing.

Although the Doctor and his companions had withdrawn out of the nave and retreated into the sanctuary, still the ghostly figures advanced unrelentingly, and still the hollow drumming boomed through the roar and smoke of the Malus.

Turlough glanced over his shoulder; the stained glass window loomed above them and scattered fragments of coloured light across the floor and their bodies, making their situation even more bizarre and unnerving. 'We're running out of places to run,' he murmured to Tegan.

'That's becoming the story of our lives,' she sighed.

Will Chandler, tucked behind Jane, peeped out at the deathly faces advancing towards him. He had seen them before. These men had been among the Puritan force which attacked the church when the great and terrible battle began. He had seen each of them cut down by Cavaliers. Yet here they were, marching up the nave, large as life and pale as death. *Marching*. He whimpered with fear.

Verney was moving slowly backwards at Will's side. 'Why don't they attack?' he asked.

'They will,' the Doctor promised. 'But in their own time.' He looked past the troopers to the Malus. Already swollen obscenely, it was swelling still further, and shuddering – and looking their way. The huge, glinting eyes were pointing directly at them. 'Now we're the Malus's last source of energy,' the Doctor said, 'it will make us sweat for as long as it can.'

10

Fulfilment

In the crypt, the trooper had remembered who he was.

He was on his feet, swaying over Willow's body. He shook his head again, trying to clear it of the dizziness which kept threatening to swamp him. Then he drew his sword and staggered towards the steps.

Their backs were to the wall. As Turlough had predicted, there were no more places for them to run to, and they were trapped.

Realising that victory was theirs for the taking, the ghostly figures stopped at the entrance to the sanctuary, close beside the archway which led to the side chapel and the steps to the crypt. With that uncanny precision they swung their hands across their bodies to the hilts of their swords. As one the troopers grasped them, and drew the swords together in a unified sweep which rasped steel on scabbard with a shrieking sound. The swords swept up into the light. Then they pointed them at the group huddled against the altar, with the colours of the stained glass window lying across them like a rainbow.

Will drew in his breath and shivered. 'I's gonna die,' he moaned.

The Doctor gripped his shoulder encouragingly. 'Be quiet, Will,' he whispered.

'He's right, Doctor.' Jane was shaking too; she could feel the edges of those swords already.

'Not yet he isn't,' the Doctor said. He was sure there

must be something he could do, but for the life of him he couldn't think what it was.

The trooper, who had remembered at last that he was supposed to be searching for the Doctor and the lost Queen of the May, came lurching and staggering up the steps from the crypt. He clattered across the side chapel, swung out through the archway – and found himself surrounded by three grey phantoms.

As he fell into their midst, three glinting swords swished through the air and joined each other around his throat.

Pinned by the swords, he stood rooted to the spot for a moment, wide eyed and bewildered. His head was still dizzy, and he tried desperately to make sense of what was happening to him. He glanced fearfully from one to another of the ghastly, grey-white faces, and his mouth opened wide with surprise.

The church, which had fallen silent with the trooper's arrival, now erupted with noise. The Malus trumpeted a triumphant roar and Tegan and Jane screamed and turned away their faces as the phantom soldiers raised their arms and swung their swords for the kill. The blades flashed and the brief, bloody, one-sided fight came to its inevitable close: the trooper shrieked in his death agony, then sank to the floor and lay face down among the debris and dust.

'Oh, no.' Tegan was shaking.

'Brave heart, Tegan.' The Doctor held her arm for comfort.

Jane was staring down the church in astonishment. Apart from the trooper lying on the ground, it was empty now. 'How could that happen?' she gasped.

'They've gone!' Turlough's voice mingled relief and amazement in equal amounts.

The Doctor nodded. 'That fight cost a lot of psychic energy,' he explained. 'The Malus needs to rest. Let's go before it recovers.'

Anxiously he herded them towards the door. They were all looking warily at the Malus: it was quiet for the moment, and seemed to be brooding, deciding on its next move. They proceeded carefully and silently, working their way down the aisle. But before they reached the door it burst open and Sir George Hutchinson came crashing through, brandishing a pistol in each hand.

His arms were outstretched and his face was twisted into a snarl. He swayed on his feet, and looked straight at the Doctor and the others.

'It is time at last!' he shouted. 'I am here, Master!'

He had not even seen them. With glazed eyes he stared up at the Malus now, a look that was almost adoration.

This was the moment the Malus had been waiting for. It throbbed. With a vast, bellowing roar of triumph it shuddered and thrust forward, pushing out of the wall to greet its servant, who now stood inside the door looking bemused and dazed as if he was uncertain what to do next.

Ben Wolsey looked at the man who had used and betrayed his village, and frowned. Then, making up his mind, he said in a quiet, unwavering voice, 'Let me deal with him.'

'He'll kill you,' Tegan said. She was looking up the dark barrels of the pistols in Sir George's hands.

But Wolsey was a man who, once he had come to a decision, was not to be put off easily. He pushed through the group and advanced slowly towards Sir George. 'Sir George used to be a man of honour,' he said, 'He played the war games in the way they were intended.'

'Forget any codes of honour Sir George might have once held,' the Doctor, at his shoulder, advised him. 'He's now completely under the influence of the Malus.'

'He's still mortal,' Wolsey said stubbornly. He fingered the hilt of his dagger.

Jane pushed through to be at his side. 'Don't be a fool, Ben.'

Wolsey turned towards her. His eyes were sad, but

133

determined. 'I have to try,' he explained. 'I feel partly responsible for what has happened here.' He turned and stepped forward again to meet Sir George.

'Ben!' Jane cried out, but her voice was drowned by the bellowing of the Malus.

Now, man to man, Ben Wolsey faced Sir George Hutchinson. An area of quiet seemed to settle around them and keep all the disturbance at bay, as though they were standing in the eye of a hurricane.

'Sir George?' Ben Wolsey said gently.

The Squire swayed uncertainly. He heard Wolsey's voice, but was unable to focus on it and decipher the jumbled sounds. He could not even find their source, because something terrible was in the way. Yet a voice had addressed him, and he had to answer. He tried, but the words would not come; his eyes bulged and he swayed on his feet.

But the pistols still pointed at Wolsey.

Will Chandler had not taken his eyes off them since the moment Sir George had entered the church. He felt nothing but hatred for this man, and now that the phantoms had gone and his old truculence had returned, the hatred was making him aggressive – even courageous.

He tugged at the Doctor's sleeve. 'Be it better Sir George be dead?' he asked.

'Not if there's another way,' the Doctor replied. Will was not convinced. He watched Ben Wolsey trying to talk sense to a madman, and shook his head. That, surely, wasn't the way.

'Sir George?' Wolsey was trying again, and endeavouring to ignore the pistols waving in front of his face. 'Do you understand me?'

The voice came to Sir George as through a dense fog. He tried again to focus on the speaker. 'Who are you?' he asked in a confused voice.

For a moment Ben Wolsey felt almost sorry for him.

'Colonel Wolsey,' he said gently. 'Ben Wolsey. Your friend.'

Finding a flaw in the determination of its servant, the Malus roared and jerked Sir George back to full attention. He pointed the guns firmly at Wolsey's head. 'Get back!' he warned. Now, impelled by the Malus, he moved steadily forward.

Wolsey was forced to retreat. Yet despite this setback he was determined to take care of Sir George himself. 'We've something to settle,' he insisted.

Sir George did not even hear him this time, because the Malus was inside his head again.

'Sir George,' the Doctor said urgently. He came forward to stand at Wolsey's shoulder. 'It's vital that you should listen.'

But Sir George kept moving forward, pressing them back. At the same time he was edging round towards his master.

The Malus roared.

The noise thundered down the crypt and reached out to Joseph Willow, who lay sprawled where he had fallen. It entered his mind like a lightning stroke.

Willow sat bolt upright, as if someone had dashed cold water over him. He drew his pistol hurriedly, then hesitated, trying to remember where he was. His head ached and he felt shaken; when he saw the gun in his hand he felt puzzled. Then the noise echoed in his ears again. It filled his head, drew him to his feet and led him across the crypt to the steps.

Sir George Hutchinson had worked round to stand in front of the Malus. The monstrous head loomed above him, jerking, shuddering, roaring constantly now and billowing dense smoke.

They had to shout to be heard above the noise. 'Listen

135

to Colonel Wolsey!' the Doctor cried. 'Concentrate your thoughts – you must break free of the Malus!'

'Free?' Sir George stabbed the pistols forward. 'Why? I'm his willing servant.'

'You're his slave,' the Doctor argued. 'He only wants you for one thing.'

The Malus roared; the noise buffeted Sir George and he staggered and swayed, utterly disorientated. 'You're mistaken,' he cried. 'He has offered me enormous power!' He tried to smile, but the pressure in his head was monstrous and his face twisted with pain.

'No!' the Doctor tried again. How could he explain? 'The Malus is here for one reason – to destroy. It's the only thing it knows how to do.'

Ben Wolsey saw the confusion on Sir George's face. The Doctor seemed to be getting through to him. 'Now listen to the Doctor,' he pleaded.

Sir George was being torn apart. He tried to hear the Doctor's words but the Malus lashed his brain and he cried out in agony. He put a hand to his head to contain the noise; he felt as if his skull was breaking open. He waved the other hand, and the pistol it still held, at the Doctor. 'I don't believe you,' he moaned.

The noise of the Malus was beginning to vibrate the whole fabric of the church. The Doctor doubled his efforts. He shouted above the raging sound: 'Without you the Malus is helpless . . . through you it feeds on the fear and anger generated by the war games. Once it is strong enough it will destroy you!'

Sir George stared wildly at the Doctor. But as his uncertainty returned, the Malus began to sheer the mind clean out of him. His face moved into a paroxysm of pain. 'No!' he screamed. He staggered, but used all his strength to recover his balance, and levelled the pistols again.

Wolsey's hand grasped the hilt of his dagger. The Doctor stepped forward to make one last effort. But as he did so, Joseph Willow appeared in the archway and crept up behind them. He had exchanged his pistol for a knife.

'Sir George,' the Doctor pleaded, 'your village is in turmoil and you're pointing your gun at a man who is a friend. That's the true influence of the Malus. Can't you feel the rage and hate inside your head? Think, man!'

The Malus roared and Sir George staggered and clutched his head again. He was grunting and moaning, and beginning to buckle under the weight of pain. 'Did you have any such feelings before you activated that thing?' the Doctor insisted.

Sir George gasped. He reeled; he was losing control of his limbs. 'I . . . don't . . .' He could find no words to express what he was feeling. The pain took him up into its web and enmeshed him. 'I . . . don't . . .' he tried again, but he could make no progress against the searing lights which blocked and burned his mind. The heavy pistol dropped out of his hand. He toppled to his knees, clutching his head with both hands.

That was the opportunity Ben Wolsey had been waiting for. He raised his dagger and moved forward for the kill.

'No!' the Doctor shouted. He dived at the big man and grasped his arm to hold him back. At the same moment Willow made his move, charging the group from behind. He took them by surprise and broke through easily, then he too, knife in hand, launched himself at Wolsey.

Although Wolsey was stronger than Willow he was hampered by the Doctor, so the two men were evenly balanced and for long moments grappled for supremacy. They gripped each other's knife arm at the wrist and the knives hung poised in the air; their arms strained and their faces trembled with effort. The Malus roared, Jane screamed, Tegan shouted; the Doctor tried to drag the struggling men away from Sir George, who was moaning and pushing himself to his feet.

It was Turlough who ended the impasse. He leaped on Willow from behind and dragged him backwards. Taking his chance, the Doctor finally overpowered Ben Wolsey and pulled him away too.

All the time they had been fighting, Will Chandler had taken no notice of them. Instead, he had been staring at Sir George, watching his struggle as he groped to his feet, watching him now as he stood dazed and swaying just in front of the gaping mouth of the Malus. In his mind, Will was seeing not Sir George but his ancestor of centuries ago, the evil man who had pressed Will into service and forced him into the battle of the church and the worst moments of his life. Will hated him for that.

And now, when Turlough dragged Willow unexpectedly in one direction and the Doctor pushed Wolsey in another, Will saw a clear pathway between them to Sir George, and something snapped inside him.

The Malus, screaming at the frustration of its plans, belched clouds of smoke and set the whole nave shaking with its noise. The roof timbers started to quiver. Pieces of plaster, shaken from their anchorage by the rumbling vibration, fell to the floor with a clattering sound. And Will, freed from the anchorage of his fear, shot out of the group like an arrow released from a bow and scuttled into the smoke billowing around the Malus and Sir George.

Verney and Jane saw him run and sensed instantly what he was about. 'No!' Verney cried. Jane shouted, 'Will, don't!' But Will did not hear them. He was running blind, possessed by a single idea – to destroy the man who had destroyed him.

Sir George could offer no resistance. His mind had been blown and he was totally confused and disoriented. Will grabbed hold of him, and as he looked up into the mad face there were tears in his eyes. 'You gonna be dead!' he yelled – and pushed him backwards with all his strength.

138

Sir George cried out as he stumbled, tripped and fell back into the wide open mouth of the roaring Malus. He disappeared from sight. There was a momentary silence and then a long, gurgling scream, suddenly cut off. Black smoke belched from the Malus, and then it fell silent, and still.

Sweating and breathing heavily, Will leaned wild-eyed against the pulpit for support. Wolsey and Willow ceased struggling; stunned by this latest event, they all looked on quietly as the Doctor approached him.

Will's fear had returned. He was appalled by what he had done. Yet he knew it was justified, and to forestall the Doctor before he could speak he looked him in the eye and shouted, 'It is better he be dead!'

The Doctor held out his hands to placate him. 'It's all right, Will,' he said quietly. 'It's all right.'

The church was heavy with smoke. Wreaths of it hung like fog around the silent pews. The Malus looked like a dead thing, as hideously ugly in death as it had been in life.

Jane Hampden ran to the Doctor. 'We must seal up the church,' she said.

Following her, Andrew Verney added, 'And we must inform the authorities. That thing has to be destroyed.'

But the Malus was not dead, or defeated yet. At Verney's words it opened its eyes wide and glared at them. And then, from deep inside its being, from far back in the wall and centuries back in time, a new noise began.

It moved rapidly towards the surface. They could hear it rolling forward and upward, gathering momentum and increasing in volume as it came, building and rushing like a wind, like a hurricane, like a banshee shrieking and wailing, like the end of the world . . . And still the noise came on.They were transfixed by the overwhelming power of it, struck dumb and frozen to the spot as the tumult grew deafening and rolled on and on, and the church began to shake before its coming like a tree bending before a great wind.

Suddenly a massive beam was dislodged from the roof timbers and crashed into the nave behind them. Blocks of stone tumbled down in clouds of dust.

That broke the spell. Their silence became uproar as the women screamed and the men cried out in fear. 'Now what?' Turlough yelled, watching the eyes of the Malus flash and roll, seeing that great head shudder. Smoke billowed from it and filled the nave with a pungent fog, so that they could scarcely see the rubble and stones and beams which toppled down around them.

And the noise was still coming.

'The Malus knows it has lost!' the Doctor shouted at the top of his voice. 'It's going to fulfil its programming and clear the ground, destroy everything it can! Come on!'

He started to run for the crypt. One by one they followed him, each dodging an avalanche of falling masonry as the Malus shook the church to its foundations. It bellowed in its death agony, writhing and twisting about as if, like Sir George, it had turned insane.

It shook and shivered, tearing itself out of the wall at last.

With the others hard on his heels the Doctor careered down the steps and across the crypt to the TARDIS. The crypt itself was shaking like the church above and pieces of the roof were breaking away.

The Doctor waited at the door of the TARDIS to count them through. One by one they ran past him – Will Chandler, Joseph Willow, Jane Hampden, Ben Wolsey, Tegan and old Andrew Verney. Turlough stayed back with the Doctor for a moment. 'Does the Malus still have the power?' he asked.

'Enough to keep Will here and level the church,' the Doctor shouted through the turmoil. 'Come along!'

Now they too ran inside the TARDIS and followed the others into the console room. The Doctor raced to the console and immediately began to hit switches, set coordinates and adjust slide controls. The TARDIS was shaking too, with the church and the crypt; at any moment they could all go up together.

'Close the door, would you?' the Doctor asked Jane. As she obeyed he slammed the master power control. Motors roared into life, the time rotor began to oscillate, and the TARDIS dematerialised, just as the roof of the crypt began to cave in. Tons of stone and timber crashed down on the spot where it had been.

Inside the church whole sections of the roof were falling down. The noise was beyond human belief as the Malus choked and pulsed and screamed, bent on the destruction of everything around it. Pillars cracked across. Now the walls of the church tower split asunder, and the tower collapsed with a roaring of its own.

The walls of the nave caved in. The wall containing the Malus crashed down upon it and in a dry, flameless explosion the Malus blew up, shooting whole sections of the church high into the air and scattering debris far and wide, even into the streets of the village.

When the last piece of rubble had clattered to the ground, when the dust had settled, when the final echo had died away – then, at last, there was silence in Little Hodcombe.

Inside the TARDIS, the motors hummed quietly.

The Doctor put his hands into his pockets and announced: 'The Malus has destroyed itself.' His voice was quiet, exhausted.

There was a general sigh of relief, although each of them was too shattered to be visibly excited by the news. A softly spoken 'Thank goodness' from Ben Wolsey summed up all their feelings.

Jane, though, still had the strength to be curious. 'Well, now that it's gone, was it a beast or a machine?' she asked.

The Doctor was moving rapidly around the console, checking that all was in order. 'It was a living thing,' he said, 're-engineered as an instrument of war and sent here to clear the way for an invasion.'

'What went wrong?' Turlough wanted to know. 'Why didn't they invade?'

'I don't honestly know,' the Doctor confessed. 'I must check to see if there's anything in the computer about it.'

Turlough wasn't satisfied with that. Frowning, he indicated the now very subdued Will Chandler standing beside him. 'If the Malus is destroyed, why is Will still here? You did say he was only a psychic projection.'

The Doctor frowned. 'Ah . . . yes,' he hedged. 'It seems I was mistaken. The Malus was able to intermingle the two time zones for a living man to pass through. It must have had incredible power.'

That's putting it mildly, Tegan thought, as she moved to her grandfather's side. 'This is the last time I pay an unexpected call on you,' she smiled.

The tired old man shook his head. With a rueful expression he took her hands in his. 'As a rule,' he said, 'the village and I are much more welcoming.'

It was a time for making peace, Ben Wolsey realised. He turned to Joseph Willow and held out his hand. 'There'll be a lot of clearing up to do, in more ways than one,' he said. 'We'll need all the help we can get.'

Willow took his proffered hand and shook it willingly. 'And with no recriminations?' he asked.

'None,' Wolsey said. 'Not on my part.'

'Nor mine,' Jane Hampden added, and shook hands too.

The Doctor, well pleased with developments, rubbed his hands with satisfaction. 'Well, that seems to be it,' he said. 'We'll drop you all off and then we can be on our way.'

'Er . . .' Turlough dropped his head to one side and indicated the quiet Will again. 'What about our friend here?'

'Ah, yes,' the Doctor nodded. 'Well, him too. 1643 isn't all that far away.'

Will's mouth dropped open. Hope sprang back into his heart.

But Tegan had something to say before the Doctor started his jaunts through time and space again. 'Aren't you forgetting something?' she asked him.

The Doctor stared at her, unable to think what it could be and unwilling, for the time being, to make the effort. He'd just begun to relax. 'Probably,' he admitted. 'It isn't unusual. I've had a very hard day.'

'We came here – correction, *I* came here to visit my grandfather,' Tegan reminded him. 'It would be nice to spend a little time with him.'

Turlough spoke up immediately in her support. 'I must admit that I wouldn't mind staying for a while.'

Jane smiled at the dumbfounded Doctor. 'You're outnumbered, seven to one,' she laughed.

The Doctor stared at them, lined up in opposition to his plan. 'I'm being bullied, coerced, forced against my will,' he complained. 'I've had enough for one day.'

Verney grinned. 'Even if you have, agree, man,' he pleaded.

'Oh, all right,' the Doctor gave in. 'But just for a little while. We've a great deal to do.'

'Good.' Now it was Turlough's turn to rub his hands with satisfaction. 'I quite miss that brown liquid they drink here.'

Will Chandler's eyes widened in a second bout of optimism. Things really were looking up. 'Ale?' he asked hopefully.

'No,' Turlough smiled. 'Tea.'

Will frowned. 'What be tea?'

143

'A noxious infusion of oriental leaves, containing a high percentage of toxic acid,' the Doctor explained.

Will turned up his nose and looked at Tegan. 'Sounds an evil brew, don't it?' he grimaced.

'True,' the Doctor said. Then he smiled and added; 'Personally, I rather like it.'

And with that he flicked the last switch which would bring the TARDIS and its passengers back to the village of Little Hodcombe, and a holiday deep in the peaceful English countryside, where nothing out of the ordinary ever happens.